DARK TRAIL

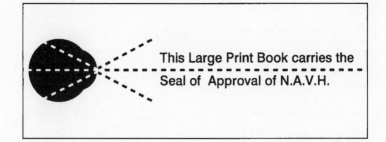

This Large Print Book carries the
Seal of Approval of N.A.V.H.

DARK TRAIL

Ed Gorman

Thorndike Press • Waterville, Maine

Published in 2005 by arrangement with Dominick Abel Literary Agency, Inc.

Thorndike Press® Large Print Western.

The tree indicium is a trademark of Thorndike Press.

The text of this Large Print edition is unabridged. Other aspects of the book may vary from the original edition.

Set in 16 pt. Plantin by Minnie B. Raven.

Printed in the United States on permanent paper.

Library of Congress Cataloging-in-Publication Data

Gorman, Edward.
    Dark trail / by Ed Gorman.
        p. cm. — (Thorndike Press large print westerns)
    Originally published: New York : M. Evans, c1990,
in series: An Evans novel of the West.
    ISBN 0-7862-7989-3 (lg. print : hc : alk. paper)
    1. Large type books. I. Title. II. Series: Thorndike
Press large print Western series.
PS3557.O759D3 2005
    813´.54—dc22   2005016540

For Peter Rabe:
peace, my friend

As the Founder/CEO of NAVH, the only national health agency solely devoted to those who, although not totally blind, have an eye disease which could lead to serious visual impairment, I am pleased to recognize Thorndike Press★ as one of the leading publishers in the large print field.

Founded in 1954 in San Francisco to prepare large print textbooks for partially seeing children, NAVH became the pioneer and standard setting agency in the preparation of large type.

Today, those publishers who meet our standards carry the prestigious "Seal of Approval" indicating high quality large print. We are delighted that Thorndike Press is one of the publishers whose titles meet these standards. We are also pleased to recognize the significant contribution Thorndike Press is making in this important and growing field.

Lorraine H. Marchi, L.H.D.
Founder/CEO
NAVH

★ Thorndike Press encompasses the following imprints: Thorndike, Wheeler, Walker and Large Print Press.

Chapter One

The cigarette had two or three good drags left and Leo Guild was happy to take them. A couple of minutes from now he was going to go bursting into the little frame farmhouse standing silver and shabby in the moonlight ten yards ahead of him. Probably there was at least one man in there guarding the prisoner with a shotgun. These might be the last drags of a cigarette Guild ever had in his life.

"You scared, Leo?" The woman who asked this stood behind the same elm tree as Guild.

"I suppose."

"That means you are."

"I am. Yes."

"You don't have to do it."

Guild took the cigarette from his lips and exhaled. He was a tall man with white hair, a black Stetson, a black suit coat, boiled white shirt, gray serge trousers, and black Texas boots. A .44 was strapped around his waist.

He smiled. "Nah, I don't have to do it, do I?"

"Don't go and get sarcastic on me, Leo."

"I could just walk back to my horse and ride out of here and you wouldn't care at all, would you, Sarah?"

"Nothin' bothers me as much as sarcasm. You know that, Leo."

Guild looked at her: the red hair, the soft pretty face, the slight but graceful body in the blue gingham dress. She wasn't exactly city but she wasn't exactly country, either. She was some fetching combination of both.

"By rights," Guild said, "I should shoot him myself when I get in there."

"It wasn't his fault, Leo. It was mine."

"You always say that."

"He wasn't the one who left you, Leo. I was."

"I didn't hear him offer to return you."

"First of all, I'm not anybody's property, Leo. And second of all —" She sighed, not wanting to hurt his feelings. "Second of all, I fell in love with Frank, Leo. I just couldn't help it."

"Leaving me for a gunfighter sure doesn't make any sense to me, Sarah." His words were tinged with anger and pain.

Now she smiled. He remembered her

when she was a teenager, smiling that way. He felt things he didn't want to feel. "That's one thing I've noticed about being thirty-five."

"What's that?"

"Almost nothing makes sense. Least of all marrying a gunfighter, I suppose." She looked at the farmhouse and smiled. "He's the little boy I never had, Leo."

Guild was out of drags. No more stalling. He dropped the cigarette to the sandy dirt and stepped on it with the pointed toe of his boot. He stood for a minute looking around at the land. In the moonlight the flat farmland was all silver and shadow. On the tops of ripe autumn corn, dew shone like fire. A nighthawk glided past the round yellow moon. A barn owl hooted lonesomely. In the surrounding hills you could smell smoky October.

"Well," Guild said, taking his .44 from his holster.

"You really don't have to do this, Leo."

He looked at her and smiled again. "Right," he said.

Guild crouched down and went through the long buffalo grass up to the front porch. He moved leftward, still crouching, gun ready.

Behind the lacy white curtains in the front window, he could see Sarah's husband Frank tied to a straight-backed chair. He was carrying on a conversation with a fat man in a plaid shirt and dungarees that had slipped aways under his considerable belly. The man held a Remington repeater in his right hand though he wasn't ready to fire it. It was just sort of dangling there from one of the man's fingers. Frank was a sweet-talker, the bastard. Now he was sweet-talking one of the men who'd captured him.

Guild couldn't see anybody else inside. He moved around the side of the house to check the horses in back. Two mounts, one a roan, the other a dun. The roan was slapping hard at flies with his tail. Given the two horses, it was clear that it was just Frank and the fat guy inside.

Guild went back around to the front of the house. Frank and the other guy were still talking. In fact, the other guy was grinning, as if Frank had just told him a funny story. That goddamn Frank. He'd always driven Guild crazy.

Guild crept up on the porch, paused, lifted up his leg, kicked in the door, and went in firing.

The air was loud with bullets ripping

into the parlor wall and hazy with the choking clouds of gunsmoke.

The fat guy thought about lifting up his Remington but Guild walked right over to him and put the .44 against his forehead.

"Please," Guild said. "I don't have anything against you and I really don't want to hurt you. You understand?"

The fat guy nodded.

"I'll be a son of a bitch," Frank Evans said.

"Untie him," Guild said to the fat guy.

"I'll be a son of a bitch."

"Now," Guild said to the man who looked dazed by all that had happened in the last minute.

The fat guy went over and untied Frank.

Guild looked around. There was a plump black stove in the archway between parlor and kitchen, new rose paper on the walls, and two wire chairs and a settee in the east corner. This was a working man's dream, cheap but new and clean.

"Your place?" Guild asked the fat guy as he untied Frank.

The fat guy, finishing, nodded.

"Tell your wife she did a good job," Guild said.

The fat guy looked at him and shrugged. "Guess she'd probably appreciate that."

Frank stood up, rubbing his wrists. "I'll be sure and tell Mr. Ingram you did a good job, Karl. Goddamned near cut off my circulation."

At that, Karl kind of grinned. Then he obviously remembered what had just happened here. "He's going to be pissed."

"I imagine so," Frank said, collecting his gun, hat, and coat from the settee. Frank Evans was short, dark, handsome in a way that was not quite pretty, and moved with a gracefulness some men found suspicious.

Frank nodded at the front door. "Sarah out there?"

"Yes."

"You hold him here while I go talk to her. I got a few things I need to say. All right?"

Guild looked at him. He'd never liked the little bastard. Never. "You giving me any choice?"

"Don't go getting that way, Leo, for Christ's sake," Frank said.

And with that, he was gone.

Guild and Karl stood in an awkward silence. "Sears, Roebuck."

"Pardon?" Guild said.

"Sears, Roebuck. That's where the missus got the furniture and stuff."

"Oh."

"I'll tell her what you said."

"Be sure to."

Karl kept staring at the .44 Guild held on him. "You his partner?"

"Frank's?"

"Yeah."

"No. Frank doesn't have a partner."

"Didn't think so. How you know him then?"

Guild looked at Karl, relishing the expression that he was about to put on Karl's face. "He stole my wife," Guild said.

Karl looked at him and whistled. "He makes a lot of people mad, don't he?"

"He sure does."

"That's why Mr. Ingram brought him out here and tied him up. He killed Mr. Ingram's brother in a gunfight."

"I'm sorry."

"Don't be. Mr. Ingram's brother was a snake."

"Oh."

"But Mr. Ingram's going to be pissed he didn't get a chance to kill Frank."

Guild laughed. "So are a lot of people."

Chapter Two

Five Years Later

It was a river town of new brick buildings and buggies, saloons and honky-tonk pianos, and pretty women in bustles and big picture hats and men in the latest Edwardian fashions stepping proudly down the dusty board sidewalks. In their minds they probably dreamed that this was Michigan Avenue in Chicago or Tyler Street in Kansas City.

Guild had been in town three weeks, living in a rooming house set beneath the sprawl of a vast tree aflame with color now that the temperature had cooled. Plump orange pumpkins had been set out on porches for Halloween a week hence.

Guild had just finished two months of guarding ore wagons up in the mountains. There had been labor union trouble, and while Guild was sympathetic to the workers, they could be just as hard-ass as the mine owners. During this time he had developed a cough. That cough was still with him as he lay awake at the breakfast hour listening to the chatter of kids in the street below, headed noisily for school.

Soon enough he'd have to start looking for work again. Good as the mine job had been, the money was mostly gone now. He didn't live high, but this time he'd treated himself to new clothes and some dental work and more than a few nights in good restaurants, ones where they served wine in a glass, not a bottle, and big porterhouse steaks with big pats of butter melting down the sides. Sometime during all this he'd turned fifty-seven.

He was recalling all this when there was a soft knock on the door. "Yes?"

"Are you decent?" asked Mrs. Tomlin.

"Some people don't seem to think so."

"Oh, you. I meant do you have clothes on?"

"Yes, I do," Guild said. Mrs. Tomlin was a widow with a quick girly smile and Guild loved to tease her.

She opened the door aways, then peeked her tiny gray head inside and saw him stretched out on the bed. "You feeling all right, Leo? Haven't seen you sleep in this late."

Then he went and coughed, just exactly

what he didn't want to do around Mrs. Tomlin, because she was sure to give him a lecture.

"Maybe you should see a doctor."

"I'm fine."

"You've been coughing since you got here."

"I'm still fine."

"I worry about you, Leo."

"I know you do and I appreciate it."

"There's breakfast left. And I'll make you some fresh toast."

"That's nice of you. But is that what you came up here to tell me?"

She flushed. "I nearly forgot." She reached in her apron and pulled out a white envelope. "This came."

"Isn't it kind of early for the mail?"

She shook her graying head. "Not the mail. A boy brought it over from the Skylark Hotel."

"I see."

She walked across the floor and handed it to Guild. As she did so, their eyes met. She was the kind of woman he liked, intelligent and purposeful but sweet, too. He took the letter.

His name was written in blue ink on the front of the envelope. He recognized the hand immediately.

He must have made a face because Mrs. Tomlin said, "Somebody you know?"

"Yes. My former wife."

"Oh." Mrs. Tomlin sounded almost hurt for some reason. "I never knew you were married."

"For a while I was."

"Is she pretty?"

He looked at her and smiled, realizing now that she was jealous. He found that oddly touching. "Not any prettier than you are, Mrs. Tomlin."

She laughed. "Aren't you the devil-tongued one, though?"

"It's the truth, Mrs. Tomlin. You're a fine-looking woman and you know it."

And then he went and spoiled this sweet moment by coughing.

"You really should —" Mrs. Tomlin began.

"See a doctor," Guild finished for her, in between his racking hacks. Then he rolled off the bed and started pulling on his boots.

"Thank you, Mrs. Tomlin."

She nodded and left, taking a sad final look at Leo bent over to his boots — a big melancholy man with blue eyes and hair very white in the small room's bright autumn sunlight.

★ ★ ★

There was a restaurant on the first floor of the hotel. It was filled with businessmen with their cigars, and proper ladies in their organdy dresses and bright paste jewelry.

In the center of the large room Sarah Evans sat staring down at her small white hands. She looked as if she might be trying to levitate them.

Guild got about the kinds of looks he'd expected from the men — a ruffian — and the ladies — an interesting if not exactly handsome man.

Sarah didn't glance up even when he reached the table. He pulled a chair out and sat down.

He'd seen her this forlorn only once before in her life — the night she'd miscarried, the night they both knew she'd never have children, despite the reassuring words of the doctor.

"Hello," Guild said.

And finally she looked up. "Hi, Leo."

"You look pretty bad."

"I feel pretty bad."

"What happened?"

"Frank."

"I figured."

"He's got this girlfriend."

"You two still married?"

She nodded. She seemed about to cry.

"That son of a bitch. The next time I see him I'm going to punch his nose in and don't goddamn try and stop me."

She laughed sadly. "The way I feel right now, I won't try to stop you, believe me."

"Where is he?"

"Up in his room on the fourth floor."

"When did this happen?"

"A few nights ago."

"The last time I saw you two, you seemed reasonably happy."

"The farmhouse that night. You went in and got him from Karl."

"Right."

She shrugged. "Things were pretty good after that. He was pretty scared that night, even if he didn't let on." Her gaze drifted back to her sweet, small hands. "Then he went back to being Frank."

The waitress came. They got another pot of coffee — she'd already polished one off all by herself — and Guild got a piece of toast. The older he got, the hungrier he got. It didn't make any sense.

"Who is she?" Guild said. "His usual?"

"She's pretty, if that's what you mean, and she's got a very fancy body."

"You still in love with him?"

"I guess so."

"How many times've you let him do this to you?"

She shrugged again. "Maybe ten."

The waitress came with the coffee and the toast, filled their cups, and left.

"She's Ben Rittenauer's girl."

"The gunnie?"

Guild whistled. "Maybe Frank's finally going to get what's coming to him." He saw that his remark had scared her. He put his big hand on her small one. "I'm sorry, Sarah. I shouldn't have said that."

She started to cry. Nothing dramatic, just silver tears in the corner of her blue eyes. She looked, just then, old and sad, and Guild remembered how much he used to love her and how scared she could get sometimes and for no good reason at all. Sometimes he felt more like her father than anything else; and many times she acted as if Frank were her son.

"Frank'll be all right," Guild said. "He always is."

"He deliberately took her from Rittenauer to make him mad." She shook her head. Her hair was gray-streaked these days. "He got tired of people telling him that Rittenauer was going to kill him someday."

"If they ever get into it, Rittenauer *will*

20

kill him," Guild said.

She looked at him and said, "Not according to Frank he won't."

Then she smiled sadly again. "You know what's going on here? Frank's almost forty. He's afraid women don't find him appealing any more and he's afraid men aren't afraid of him. Taking Rittenauer's girl helps him out both ways. He's betting Rittenauer won't call him on this."

"She must be some girl to let herself be picked off this way."

This time Sarah reached across and touched Guild's hand. "Sort of the way Frank picked me off. Me leaving you for him and all?"

"I wasn't exactly a perfect husband."

"I wish I hadn't done it that way, Leo. I hope you know that."

"I know that now. I guess I didn't then. And hell," Guild said, "maybe there's no easy way to do that anyway, to leave somebody. Maybe the way you did it was the only way it could be done."

She said, "You know why I sent that letter over to your sleeping room?"

"You want me to go see him."

"If you would."

Guild stared at her. "You really want him back?"

"I'm pretty pathetic, I know."

"You know better than that, Sarah."

Then Guild lit a cigarette, and they talked some about him going upstairs and seeing her husband, Frank.

And Guild said, finally, "Aw, hell, Sarah, you really want me to go up there?"

Chapter Three

The corridors were carpeted in red. The mahogany doors of each room were shined fine and the brass doorknobs polished bright. As he passed down the hallway, Guild heard small snippets of lives behind each door: a married couple snapping at each other here, an old man coughing up phlegm there, and the last a woman with a pretty voice singing "Beautiful Dreamer" to an infant she was apparently rocking in her arms. The infant made happy sounds as the woman sang on.

The room he wanted was at the end of the hall. There was a fire exit door on the back wall and a window that looked down on an alley. Two black men were loading a buckboard with crates from the back of a store, and they were laughing about something secret as they worked.

Guild put his ear to the door. What he heard made him walk back down the hall aways. He felt almost ashamed listening to the noises they made. This sort of thing was their business. He was just glad that Sarah hadn't come along. It would be rough, hearing them go at it that way.

He gave them ten minutes before trying again. He walked back to the door and put his ear to it.

Just then an impressive-looking man with white muttonchop sideburns and an expensive Edwardian suit came out of a room down the hall. He saw Guild there, pressing his ear to the door. Guild blushed. He started to explain and then decided the hell with it. The man had already made up his mind about what sort of person Guild was anyway.

They were done making noise. Guild knocked.

"Who is it?" Frank Evans said.

"Guild."

"Leo?"

"Yes."

"I'll be a son of a bitch."

"Who is it, sweetheart?"

"Leo Guild."

"Who's that?"

"Old friend of mine."

Which wasn't exactly true, Guild thought, but now wasn't the time to worry about that.

He could hear them scrambling into their clothes now, buttons snapping shut, boots being jerked on.

Frank Evans opened the door.

The first thing Guild noticed was his hair, how it had gone heavily salt-and-pepper. And the second thing he noticed was that Frank held a Colt right in Guild's face.

"Sorry, Leo. Just had to be sure." Frank dropped the gun.

"Same goddamn Frank as always."

Frank paid no attention. "Come on in, Leo, and meet my sweetheart."

She sat at a dressing table, combing long lustrous red hair into a fancy pile on top of a well-shaped head rising from a long, white neck. She was not at all what Guild had expected. She was elegant and beautiful. She wore a green organdy dress. In the mirror he saw that she had green, intelligent eyes and a soft, friendly smile. Guild felt sorry for Sarah. This wasn't the chippie she'd described. This was a decent woman, at least judging by appearances.

"Good morning, Mr. Guild."

"Good morning."

She patted white powder on her face with a puff. Just the right faint amount. "Would you care to join us for breakfast?"

"No, thanks, miss."

"We'd be happy to have a guest."

"All the same, miss," Guild said. He'd taken off his hat and was picking at its brim with his fingers.

She stood up. She was tall and most intimidating. The organdy rustled as she went over and gave Frank a kiss on the cheek. "I'll go for a walk for awhile then meet you downstairs. I know you two want to talk."

"Thanks, sweetheart." As he said this, Frank winked at Guild, as if he were bragging about what a find she was.

"Nice to meet you, Mr. Guild," the woman said at the door.

"Nice to meet you, too," Guild said.

She nodded and was gone.

A long moment after she had closed the door and could be heard walking down the hall, Frank said, "Sarah sent you, didn't she?"

"Yes."

"Goddamn her, Leo. Goddamn her anyway."

Frank wore black pants and a starched white shirt that still needed a collar. He paced. He moved quick like a kid, but now there were lines in the almost pretty face and around his eyes.

"I hear she's Rittenauer's woman."

He stopped pacing and looked at Guild.

"You know something I don't understand, Leo?"

"What's that?"

"Why you care so much about Sarah? After what she did to you, I mean."

"She's a good woman."

"She slept with me while she was still married to you."

"I wasn't the easiest man to live with."

"Didn't it hurt, what we did to you?"

Guild tried not to think about it. He couldn't ever remember crying in quite the way he had in those days, crying so hard in the solitary night that he felt as if he'd vomit. He'd traveled wide and far in those days — up into the mountains and then along down the river, into cities bright on the plains at night, and villages lazy and happy in the sunlight, but the pain had been always with him, always. How he'd hated them in those days, lying Sarah and quick-smiling Frank. He'd even in the longest and blackest nights planned somehow to murder them, but he never had, of course, and in the passing of years the rage had gone, and he was even able to find happy memories amidst the grief. Then when he'd seen her five years ago, when she had dragooned him into getting Frank out of that farmhouse, he'd forgiven them all, Sarah and Frank for betraying him, and himself for not being the husband Sarah had deserved.

To Frank now he said, "She loved you, Frank."

Frank sighed. "This isn't easy for me, Leo."

"I can see that. Nice hotel room. Beautiful woman. It's probably real hard work."

"You know what I mean."

"No, I don't know what you mean."

"It's just —" and he started pacing again. "You know how some people get old and other people don't?" Before Guild could say anything, "She thinks because my dad was a farmer, that's what I should be. There's some family land in Missouri. She wants me to take it over and raise corn and cattle."

Guild pointed to Frank's face. "You taken a look in the mirror lately?"

"What's that supposed to mean?"

"You still think you're this cute little kid, Frank. And you're not. You're getting to be as old as the rest of us."

Frank nodded at Guild's white head. "At least I'm not as old as you, Leo."

Guild sighed. "She loves you, Frank. And she's a damned good woman."

"I know she's a good woman, Leo. You

don't have to tell me that."

"You could have dinner with her tonight."

"I've got dinner tonight, Leo. With Beth."

Guild shook his head, went over to the window. In the sunlight the railroad tracks almost glowed. "I'm told Rittenauer's coming in tonight," he said without turning around.

"I'm not afraid of Ben Rittenauer, Leo. Just in case you're trying to scare me."

Guild turned around and faced Frank. He wanted to slap him around, but he knew it would do no good. "You should be afraid of him, Frank."

"He's a punk."

"He'll kill you, Frank."

"All he's ever fought are old men."

"You're an old man now, Frank. At least for a gunny."

Frank took an Ingram pocket watch from his trousers. "I've got to go meet Beth now, Leo."

"You remember what I said."

"You remember what *I* said. Ben Rittenauer doesn't scare me."

Guild walked over to the door, put a hand on the fancy brass knob. "It won't last long, you know. You and Beth."

"Maybe. Maybe not."

"And there's no guarantee that Sarah will be there waiting for you."

"That's my problem, Leo. Not yours."

"A nice spot in Missouri would work out real nice."

Frank grinned. "It sure could, Leo. When I get to be an old man. But not now. Not right now."

Guild turned the knob and opened the door. He'd said all there was to say.

Behind him, Frank said, "Tell her I appreciate everything, Leo."

Guild said, "I don't think that's what she wants to hear, Frank."

He left.

Chapter Four

Ben Rittenauer enjoyed train rides. He liked the way the pictures inside the frame of the window kept changing, green bluff to flinty mountain, rushing river to piney foothill, day into night. In his lap he had a big red apple and a pocket knife for paring off a white chunk of the fruit every once in awhile.

Sometimes he got up and went to the back of the car and stood on the clattering deck. He liked the noise and the sense of speed and the wind in his face. He liked the smell of grease from underneath and the stream of coal smoke from the locomotive ahead.

He got up and went to stand on the deck now, holding on tight to the railing because this particular section of road bed was rough; a man could get pitched off before he knew it. The area surrounding him now was mostly bluff, firs stretching steep all the way up to the horizon and deer roaming the long dusty buffalo grass that had

31

turned brown in the slanting autumn sunlight.

The big thing was not to think about Beth. She'd done this in Waco, in Ponca City, in St. Louis, and now she'd done it again. He hated the word "whore" — it being what his father had always called his mother during the worst of their arguments — but he could think of no other word that applied here. Whore.

He listened to the rattling rails and sucked in the scent of pines lying just beneath the coal smoke. He felt the first chill of autumn, apple cider weather being the way he usually thought of it. He thought again, miserably, of Beth.

He stayed out on the deck a few more minutes, and then went back inside to his seat and tried to get some sleep.

It was dusk when Rittenauer pulled into the city. A fat conductor carrying a lantern walked up and down the depot platform, hurrying new passengers aboard. A black man offered to carry Rittenauer's leather bag, but Rittenauer shook his head. He'd always felt foolish being waited on this way.

Downtown he saw streetlights to rival those in Chicago, saw sparkling black buggies and surreys, and women in picture hats and wide evening smiles. Shop windows were filled with all the latest items. When he saw the jeweler's he thought of Beth. How she loved to look at jewelry.

On the corner of a dark street he found a hotel named the Bredsford Arms. It was new and had three floors; quick white boys carried your bags and made irritating small talk as they preceded you up to your room.

His boy, who was maybe eighteen, kept looking at him all the way up the stairs to the second floor. Finally, he said, "Excuse me, mister, but you sure do look familiar."

"I do, huh?"

"Yessir." The boy, obviously observant, took note of Rittenauer's gaze. "I hope I'm not making you mad, sir."

"No, son, you're not. But if you don't turn around and watch where you're going, you're going to trip on one of those stairs and break your goddamned neck."

The boy grinned. "Yessir."

They reached the second floor. The narrow hallway smelled of shaving soap and cigar smoke and, more faintly, of sweet perfume.

The bed was soft but not too soft and the window overlooking the street below was small but not too small. How Rittenauer loved to look out windows.

The boy set Rittenauer's leather bag down on the bed and said, "Ben Rittenauer."

Rittenauer sighed. "Do you win some sort of prize now?"

"Sir?"

"For guessing my name right."

The boy's face got red. "I didn't mean to make you mad, sir."

Rittenauer sighed again shaking his head, and went over to the window. He stared down at the street. "Do whatever you do, kid, and then get the hell out of here."

"Yessir."

Rittenauer had shot three men in fair fights before he was thirty-two years old. This had made him, in a small part of the country, a "personage," as journalists liked to say. But Rittenauer was tired of being a personage and tired of all the goddamn kids like this one who were stupid enough to believe that Rittenauer was somebody special.

All he wanted was Beth back, and to take care of Frank Evans.

"I didn't mean anything by that, sir."

"I know, son. I shouldn't have snapped at you like that." He turned around and flipped the kid a shiny quarter. "Where can you get a good meal in this town?"

"The Ames House. Real good chops and steaks."

"Fine. Thank you."

"You be needing anything else, sir?"

"No. Nothing."

The kid paused. "You ever give autographs, Mr. Rittenauer?"

"No, son, I don't."

"Oh." The kid looked even younger and dumber, in his bandleader jacket and his vastly disappointed small-town frown. "I see."

Rittenauer turned back to the window.

The kid left.

Sometimes he imagined he could hear the ghosts of the room. All the traveling salesmen, all the happy and unhappy married couples, all the lonely young men and lonely young women. He could hear prayers and curses and laughter and tears, all in the pretty papered walls of this room.

He lay on the bed now, resting from the train journey, wondering just how many such rooms he'd been in since Beth had left him a year ago?

Ben Rittenauer had looked for her everywhere. He took every tip, every suggestion, every "logical deduction," and followed it down.

And always it led him to a room like this, where he would lay on the bed and hear vague voices rumbling in the rooms on either side of him, and where he could hear the ghosts of roomers past on the dusty air.

Finally, he slept. Not long or well but enough to make him feel a little better when he woke up.

He stripped down to his pants and then took the wash bowl on the bureau and carried it down to the bathroom to get fresh water. He brought it back, shaved and washed under his arms, and put on some of the stuff Beth had bought him. He slapped it on; it stung and felt good at the same time. And certainly it smelled good.

He went over to the bed and put on his shirt and his gun and his jacket. And then he went out into the waiting night.

Chapter Five

It took Guild twenty minutes to talk Sarah out of her room and over to a combination restaurant and tavern called The Crowing Rooster. When she was upset, Sarah went for days without leaving her room and ate only rarely. She also bit her fingernails with such ferocity that it was painful to watch. When you looked at her hands, her fingers were bloody stumps.

She looked pretty in the glow of the Rochester lamp, sitting across from Guild. She would not order for herself — "Just coffee's fine, Leo, honest" — so he'd ordered for her, a porterhouse steak that he said he'd split with her because they were expensive, and sweet potatoes and corn on the cob. When she wouldn't eat, Guild said, "I'm not going to eat till you do."

"You need your food, Leo," she said.

"You heard what I said," he said. She frowned and dug into her food. While she didn't eat all of it she did eat most of it, and that made Guild feel a lot better.

He was just finishing his last bite of the butter-melted steak when a stout man in a good, dark suit came over and stood next to the table.

"I understand you're Leo Guild," he said. Guild looked up at the man, swallowed down the steak, and nodded. The man was jowly and had a mustache, and a nose too small for his moon face. He set a small white business card on the table and said, "I understand that you know Frank Evans."

Guild glanced over at Sarah. "Yes, I know Frank. This happens to be his wife, matter of fact."

The man took his hat off and nodded. "You'd be Sarah then; Sarah Evans."

Sarah nodded. She looked nervous. What the hell was all this about?

"Most pleased to meet you, ma'am," the man said. Then he turned his attention back to Guild. "Could you possibly meet me at the Swenson Tap Room at ten tonight?"

"I suppose. Mind telling me what it's about?"

The man's eyes strayed to Sarah, then back to Guild. "I'd rather wait till then, if you don't mind. No offense, ma'am."

Guild picked up his card. "Hollister."

"Yes."

"Ten?"

38

"Ten o'clock, Mr. Guild."

Guild put the card in his shirt pocket. "Ten o'clock it is, Mr. Hollister."

"He'll come back, Leo. He always does."

"I'm not sure that's the question."

She sighed. "You mean, maybe I shouldn't *want* him back?"

"Exactly."

"I love him."

"You think you do anyway."

"Oh, no, Leo, I know I do. Honest."

As they walked through the downtown and then the park and then along the moon-silvered river, they could see their breath as they talked. Everything was silver-touched with hoarfrost and moon-light, and the lone roaming dogs of the night looked cold. The horses in the livery made contented sounds in their snug blankets and hay, and the distant roaring train sounded fierce and purposeful hurtling across the empty prairie.

"I'll tell him I'll give him just one more chance."

"Umm-hmm."

"No call to get sarcastic."

"I'm not getting sarcastic. I'm just saying you've given him one last chance a lot of different times."

"But this time he'll understand."

"Why this time?"

"Because he's getting older, Leo. He's got to understand that. A girl like Beth . . . if Ben Rittenauer can't hold her, how can Frank hold her?"

"I wouldn't bet Frank believes that."

They were back at her hotel. The lobby was filled with geezers reading newspapers and *The Police Gazette*, smoking cigars, and chewing tobacco, which they deposited in impressive brown arcs into tarnished brass spittoons. Pimples of steam covered the front display window.

"You're really a good friend, Leo, and I appreciate it. Sometimes I wish I hadn't —"

But he put his hand to her soft warm lips and stopped her from saying it. He knew she didn't mean it — it was just the moment and her grief speaking — and in some way it would be painful to hear her say it, so he stopped her.

"You get some sleep," he said.

"That Hollister."

"I was thinking about him, too."

"Wonder how he knows Frank."

"I don't know."

"And he even knew my name."

"I noticed."

"What do you think he wants?"

"I don't have any idea."

"You'll tell me?"

"I will."

"You promise?"

"I promise."

"Maybe I should never have left you, Leo."

So she'd said it after all.

"You go get some sleep, Sarah."

"You'd never treat a woman this way."

So he leaned over and kissed her on the cheek and said, "Just try and relax a little, Sarah."

"Leo, I —"

"Really," he said. "Just relax."

And then he was gone, footsteps in the gloom moving briskly toward the saloons and taverns along the river.

At ten o'clock Guild walked into the Swenson Tap Room. The lights ran to kerosene lanterns, and the atmosphere to the kind of leather-seated opulence the more successful drummers not only enjoyed but insisted on. The place was only a few blocks from the depot and likely did a lot of business with travelers. There was a man in a dark and conservative suit at a piano. A woman with high-piled hair and a nice bosom framed in a low-cut dress greeted Guild as he came in. There was nothing coy about her. Her smile was pleasant, perhaps even sincere, but utterly without sexual promise, and Guild admired her for that.

When he told her he was looking for Hollister, she nodded and led him to the back of the place where a large booth was hidden behind massive burgundy-colored drapes. She parted the drapes and peeked in, saying, "Mr. Guild is here."

A low, masculine voice rumbled something. She closed the drapes and looked up at Guild. "Could you give them a minute?"

"Sure."

"Thank you." She nodded to the front door. "I need to get back."

Guild nodded. She left.

He stood there looking over the place — the huge cloud of smoke that had settled in the center of the room, the nicely dressed clientele, the pinochle game going on over in the corner. He did not belong in a place like this. It brought to mind the fact that he was by trade a farmer and rancher and now bounty hunter, that he was not educated well and did not always dress well. He felt ashamed of himself and then angry at himself for feeling ashamed. If Hollister had not invited him, Guild would never have come into a place like this.

The curtains parted. Two men sat at a round poker table. One was Hollister. The other was a tall, white-haired man with a long white mustache and pitiless blue eyes. He wore a gray suit that lent him the air of a Confederate general. He was probably forty.

He sat there quite frankly taking Guild's measure. Guild couldn't tell if the man was impressed with what he saw. He was the sort of man you'd never know anything about unless he chose to tell you, and that wasn't very likely.

Hollister said, "Mr. Guild, this is Tom Adair."

Adair put a long arm out. Guild shook his hand. The man had a strong, dry grip.

"And you're drinking what, Mr. Guild?" Hollister asked.

"A shot of whiskey and a schooner would be fine."

"Any particular brand?"

"Whatever they've got."

Hollister's eyes showed a kind of amused tolerance for Guild.

Once they were all seated and the barmaid had set their drinks in front of them and drawn the curtain, Hollister said, "Do you know who Tom Adair is, Mr. Guild?"

Guild looked at Adair. "I've heard the name. But right off I couldn't tell you where."

"Richest man in this river valley," Adair said. "I have farms, two bauxite mines, several retail stores, and a half interest in the short-line railroad that serves this state and the four contiguous states. I also have a lot more, but I've probably done a pretty good job of impressing you already, haven't I, Mr. Guild?"

There was no hint of irony in the man's voice.

"You'd think so, wouldn't you?" Guild said.

Tom Adair leaned forward. There was something predatory about his face up close in the glow of the Rochester lamp. "I also have a lot of important friends."

"I'm sure you do."

As if he were a vaudevillian taking over his part of the act, Hollister asked, "Have you ever studied history, Mr. Guild?"

"Not as much as I should have."

"Well," Hollister said, "if you ever read about the Roman emperors, you'll find that they all had one problem in common." Guild didn't say anything. Hollister looked at Adair and then continued. "They had a difficult time keeping their friends — and

44

all the other citizens of Rome — amused. You're familiar with the Coliseum and the games?"

Guild nodded.

"Well, during the reign of each emperor, the citizens and friends of the court got bored with the games and demanded new pleasures."

"I see."

"Have you ever heard of Tiberius?"

"I'm afraid not."

Adair took over once more from Hollister. "He had a particularly bad problem, Mr. Guild. His palace courtiers were so bored with the games that they began to dislike Tiberius personally. He had to come up with something that was really unique."

Hollister said, "So that's why he came up with the idea of the bear and the baby."

"The bear and the baby?"

"He'd have his soldiers capture great black bears from the mountains and then bring them to Rome."

Guild wasn't sure he wanted to hear the rest of this.

Hollister continued, "Then he'd gather the elite citizens of Rome along the river's edge. Before their eyes, he'd have the bears killed in a very brutal fashion, after which

45

he'd have them gutted and laid open."

"I see."

Adair said, "Not yet you don't, Mr. Guild. Do you know what he'd put inside the bears?"

Guild said nothing. Knowing what was coming next, he felt sick.

Leaning even farther forward so that Guild could feel the man's spittle spray across his face, Adair continued. "He'd take the youngest infants of the palace slaves and have them sewn inside the empty bellies of the bears. The babies were alive inside there. You could hear them crying and screaming."

"And then the guards would take the bears and hurl them into the water," Hollister took over, "and the crowd would watch the bears sink with the babies drowning inside."

"And it turned Tiberius' fortune around. He was known, for the rest of his life, as one of the great games-givers of Roman history," Adair said.

Guild knocked his whiskey back. He wanted to reach across and slap Adair. Hollister was too much of a toady to even bother with.

"What do you think of that, Mr. Guild?" Hollister asked.

"I think Tiberius should have been killed. With somebody's hands."

Hollister laughed. "Now don't go and get moral on us, Mr. Guild. We told you that story for a reason."

The barmaid came, and Hollister ordered another round for the three of them.

When the barmaid had gone, Adair said, "Important people tend to get bored easily, Mr. Guild. They're too sophisticated to put up with things that would amuse ordinary people."

"Tomorrow night there's a birthday party out at the ranch for Mr. Adair. He'll be forty-two," said Hollister.

"I haven't been able to come up with any event that would really please my friends," Adair said. "Till now, that is."

"What he's got in mind is a real honest-to-God gunfight held right at the ranch," Hollister said.

Adair said, smiling for the first time, "And I'm willing to pay you two thousand dollars to deliver the two men to my place tomorrow night. I'm talking about Frank Evans and Ben Rittenauer, Mr. Guild. And you can tell them for me that the winner gets ten thousand dollars in good Yankee cash. Now how does that sound, Mr. Guild?"

"Not interested," Guild said.

"Not interested?" Hollister said. "In two thousand dollars?"

"That's right. Not interested."

And with that he stood up.

"I appreciate the drinks, gentlemen."

"You're actually going to turn down two thousand dollars?" Adair asked.

"I am," Guild said.

"You don't have to take part in any of it, Mr. Guild. All you have to do is deliver them," Hollister said.

"I realize that."

"And you still won't do it?"

"That's right," Guild said, taking a certain pleasure in frustrating two men as sure of themselves as these two. "I won't do it."

"Well, I'll be damned," Adair said. "A bounty hunter with scruples."

Guild touched his hat in a farewell salute and left.

Chapter Six

Ben Rittenauer stood in the street across from the hotel and looked up at the fourth floor window, the one where the desk clerk said Beth and Frank Evans were staying. A kerosene lamp burned beyond the gauzy white curtains, and once or twice he'd glimpsed the silhouette of a woman passing quickly by the window. He'd felt sick and exhilarated alike. Twice a uniformed policeman walked by the corner where Rittenauer stood, taking suspicious note of the stranger standing there.

It was getting late now. Everything but a few saloons was closed up. Fog in silver tatters floated down the streets. Inside the fog you could hear footsteps on the board sidewalks, and the occasional sounds of lovers laughing about something to each other. A huge clock mounted on a pole outside the jeweler's chimed loudly at midnight. Far away a single surrey worked its way home, the hoofslaps of its one horse lonely in the silver gloom. The fog made everything dreamy and unreal. Rittenauer stood there staring up at the fourth floor window, having absolutely no idea what to do with not only this evening but with his entire life. Being heartsick made him like this, crazed and frantic in a quiet way.

The third time he passed by, the policeman said, "You got business here?"

"I'm just getting some air."

"You keep looking up at the hotel."

"I suppose I do."

"I'd like to know why."

Rittenauer sighed. "There's a woman up there."

"Oh?"

"A woman I know."

"Why don't you go up and see her then?"

"I can't."

"Why not?"

"She's with somebody."

The policeman raised his eyes to the fourth floor, third window from the right. The silhouette was there again. Beth.

"Yeah, she might complain," the policeman said.

"Complain?"

"Look down and see you standing here and complain. You've been here a long time. She's apt to get frightened."

The policeman, who had a belly beneath his blue uniform with the smart gold buttons, wore a wide creaking holster and a pair of stylish fawn-pink gloves. He tugged the gloves on tighter now, as if he were going to punch Rittenauer. "You don't take a hint very well, do you?"

"Huh?"

"I'm asking you to move on."

"Oh."

The policeman stared at him. "Now."

"Oh. Right."

Rittenauer took one more look up at the window. He felt sick to his stomach. She was so close. In a minute or two he could be at her room. He had so many things to say. Soft and loving things, hard and bitter things. He wanted to hold her and feel her and taste her. He wanted her to be the way she'd been back in the days when he'd been the peacekeeper in the infamous Kansas City saloon where everybody from the Earp brothers to Wild Bill took time to get drunk.

Being a gunfighter wasn't in itself lucrative, but when you were a gunfighter of some repute, rich and powerful people always wanted to hire you for something or other. Rich and powerful people seemed to like gunfighters as much as young kids did. You could sit with a rich man and he'd buy

51

you steaks and drinks all night, and maybe even get you a woman or two. Just as long as you kept playing hard at being the tough and fearless gunfighter he wanted you to be. You never told him about the night before a gunfight, how you paced and prayed and sweated, or about the aftermath sometimes, how you couldn't quit shaking till way into the next day. They wanted to believe that you were brave and fearless, and so that's how you played it for them.

"You hear me?" the policeman said. "About moving on?"

Rittenauer, moving his gaze from the window to the policeman's doughy, middle-aged face, said, "I hear you."

And then Rittenauer, too, was just invisible footsteps on the board sidewalk in the silver floating fog.

He didn't even really look at the place or anybody in it while he downed three shots of whiskey and two glasses of beer. When he saw that one drunk was in the process of recognizing him, he turned his face away. He was in no mood to amuse hayseeds with tales of gun battles.

Rittenauer was in the place an hour. He didn't feel any better when he left but he did have an idea anyway. Tonight, this very moment, he was going to speak his piece, and if Beth didn't like it or Frank Evans didn't like it, he didn't give a damn.

He walked straight over to the hotel.

Except for an old man sleeping in a chair, the lobby was empty. The young desk clerk was reading a magazine when Rittenauer walked past.

The desk clerk looked up. "Hey."

"Pardon me?"

"You got business upstairs?"

"Yes, I do."

"What sort of business?"

"Seeing a friend."

"What friend?"

Rittenauer walked over to the desk. "Son, do you know who I am?"

"No."

"Good."

"Good?"

"Yes. Because if you did know who I was, you wouldn't be taking that tone with me."

"Oh, I wouldn't, huh?"

"No, you wouldn't. I'm Ben Rittenauer."

And it worked. Just like that it worked. Rittenauer didn't even have to drop his hand to the .44 strapped around his waist. He just spoke his name and watched the reaction.

"You really are?" The desk clerk now sounded as young as he looked.

"I really am."

"I'll be dogged."

"Now I'd like to go upstairs if you don't mind."

"All I ask is you don't get me in trouble. Don't shoot anybody or anything."

"Right."

"I'm really glad to meet you, Mr. Rittenauer."

"Right."

Rittenauer went upstairs.

Beyond the doors were the sounds of coughing, of nightmares, of snoring. Beyond the doors drummers lay lonely, long-married couples lay sleeping with a familiar hand planted fondly on a familiar hip, and young married couples lay making love. He felt separate from all this. He had his anger now, his need to tell her everything that was constantly exploding in his head and heart.

He found their door and put his head to it and listened. And heard nothing. They were sleeping.

He wanted to ease open the door, go in there and slap the hell out of Evans, and then take her by the arm and drag her down the stairs and out of this place forever.

His hand touched the doorknob. Started to turn it. His heart hammered. He was eager to get inside.

And then he heard the footsteps creaking down the hall. He turned to see this slender and very pretty woman standing there. She had an odd, almost crazy smile on her face and she said, "I see we both got the same idea."

"Ma'am?"

"Go in there and tell them what we think of them. Make them just as miserable as they've made us."

"Ma'am?"

The woman took a few steps closer to him. "You're Ben Rittenauer. I'm Sarah Evans. I'm Frank's wife."

"Oh," he said. "Oh."

Chapter Seven

Guild was halfway back to his boarding-house when he heard footsteps coming up fast behind him on the board sidewalk. He touched his hand to his .44, ready to draw and fire if necessary. The fog, thick and chill, unnerved him.

"Mr. Guild! Mr. Guild!"

The footsteps got faster. He could hear an overweight human being panting now from exertion. From the fog there emerged the shape of Adair's hired man. Hollister.

Hollister got his hand on Guild's shoulder and slowed him down. Hollister's chest was heaving so hard, Guild was afraid the man was going to have a heart attack.

"Mr. Adair thinks we misjudged you," Hollister panted, swatting silver fog from his face the way he would gnats. In the shadows from the streetlight, Hollister's face looked fat and sweaty.

"He does, huh?"

"He said that he didn't know you were a man of honor."

"A man of honor. I see."

"Like himself, that is."

This time Guild didn't bother to be sarcastic. He just snorted. "Is that what Adair is, a man of honor?"

Hollister looked hurt, as if Guild had said something dirty about Hollister's father. "That's how he likes to think of himself, Mr. Guild."

"I'm still not interested in your deal, Hollister."

"He said he wants to give you till morning to reconsider."

"I won't change my mind."

"Then he'll have me talk to them myself — Evans and Rittenauer, I mean."

"Then you talk to them."

"They're going to fight anyway, Mr. Guild. You might as well make two thousand dollars on it. You can make it easier for everybody involved."

"No, thanks."

Hollister paused and looked carefully at Guild. "I'm told Evans' wife used to be your wife."

"You're not going to get to me that way, either, Hollister."

"You shouldn't have any love for Frank Evans."

"I don't."

"Then why wouldn't you want to see him go up against Ben Rittenauer. Ben may very well kill him."

"If they want to fight, that's up to them. I just don't think they should do it for the amusement of a bunch of railroad barons."

Hollister sighed. "They're not such bad folks when you get to know them, Mr. Guild."

"Maybe not. But I don't plan to meet them to find out."

"Who do you think will win?" Hollister asked.

"Evans or Rittenauer?"

"Yes."

Guild shrugged. "Hard to say. Evans is faster, Rittenauer's a better shot. They're probably pretty even."

"Then it should be a very good fight."

"Your friend Adair will get his blood money's worth, if that's what you're really asking."

"One of those men is going to make a nice profit that day. Whichever one of them gets out alive, that is."

"Good night, Hollister."

In a moment, out of the circle of lamplight, Guild became nothing more than footsteps on the boards in the fog.

"Good night, Mr. Guild. You've got till

morning to change your mind."

Guild just kept walking.

He sat by the window, at the table. Frank Evans wore trousers but no shirt and no shoes. Before him on the table was a stack of greenbacks, a modest stack. In the summer past he had traveled with a carnival, doing fast-draw exhibits and taking part in a laughable presentation about gunfighters put on by an ersatz Southern colonel who went by the name Fitzsimmons. The money had been good and Beth had liked the celebrity that attached to being Frank Evans' girl.

That was the odd thing about her. For all her beauty, for all the splendid manner she affected, she was really a naive young woman. The show was tawdry, really, but Beth didn't seem to notice. She just liked the way the townspeople swirled around her, asking her questions about Frank and other gunfighters. After a show, she always made Frank go for a walk in town with her, her arm in his, watching people point at them and smiling.

The curious thing was, when they were alone, she never asked him about gunfighting, about what it was really like, about the early years when he'd been

59

earning his reputation. And she never asked about money. She just seemed to assume it would always be coming in. At least that was how she spent it. So many clothes; so much time in front of the mirror.

That reminded him of the one thing he missed about his wife, Sarah. Her wisdom. Bring any sort of problem to Sarah, and in her quiet, almost brooding way she could solve it for you. But that was part of Sarah's problem, at least as Frank saw it. Her drabness. There was no fun left in her. She was more like his sister or mother than his lover. Beth was the opposite. The very opposite. Beth was a prize. Beth was the woman all the other men envied. Beth was the girl who made you feel as young as you'd once been. Beth was the girl who made you just a little better than the other men. Beth was the measure of your manhood. And as he neared forty, he realized that he must keep Beth at all costs.

But lately he hadn't been able to sleep well. He'd sit up at night in their succession of hotel rooms, counting his money and counting it yet again, as if it might have magically multiplied since the last time he'd counted it. Winter would have to come and then spring before the carnival was ready to roll again, before he was collecting a steady paycheck again. He could have gotten a regular job somewhere, he supposed, but he knew that both Beth and he himself would have been disappointed if he did. Frank Evans couldn't work at an ordinary job like an ordinary man. Just couldn't.

Beth rolled over now, snoring softly and wetly. She had a way of sleeping with one hand flung across her face like a tiny girl. Standing above her at such times he found her so adorable that he was afraid of her . . . of losing her . . . of not having the prize other men envied.

This time he didn't get up to look. He just stared out the window at the fog. Seen from four floors up, the stuff was like a silver river floating through the midnight town, the moon a round golden disc behind the haze.

He sighed, and counted his money once again.

They found a place over by the railroad tracks where a respectable woman could go without being embarrassed.

The place was crowded and smoky and the service pretty bad. Ben Rittenauer ended up getting them their own coffee

61

and bringing it back, along with cream and sugar.

They sat in a back booth and sipped their coffee. Finally Sarah said, "Have you ever seen them together?"

"Ma'am?"

"Seen them arm in arm walking down the street?"

"Oh. No. I guess I haven't."

"They look good."

He shrugged. "I suppose they do."

"Frank's hair is getting gray, but he's still a good-looking man."

"I've never thought about it before but I guess he is."

"And Beth is certainly a beautiful woman."

"You won't get any argument about that."

Sarah lifted her cup and blew gently across the dark surface. The coffee shimmered, like a pond on which you were skipping a stone. "I tried to do what you did," she said.

"Oh?"

"The other day I marched right up to their room and was all prepared to go in there and give them a big speech."

"But you didn't?"

"No. At the last minute I decided that I

had more pride than that."

"I'm glad you came along tonight. And stopped me, I mean."

Sarah stared at him. "You mind if I ask you something, Mr. Rittenauer?"

"How about calling me Ben."

"Ben, then."

"Be my guest. Ask away."

"Do you want her back?"

"Sure."

"You say that pretty quickly."

"Why wouldn't I? I love her and I want her back."

"Has she ever left you before?"

Just then a group of men at the counter got loud over some joke. The oppressive smoke from cigarettes and cigars, and the smell of grease from the grill began getting to Ben.

Rittenauer said, "I know what you're trying to tell me."

"And what would that be?"

"That she's done this to me before with other men and that she'll do it to me again."

"That's right. And Frank will do it to me again, too."

Rittenauer stirred more sugar into his cup. He had already put four spoonfuls in there. "How long you been with Frank?"

"Sixteen years."

Rittenauer whistled. "Long time."

"You're planning on killing him, aren't you?"

"I have to admit I've thought about it," he said.

"He's fast."

"He's fast, but he's not that fast."

"You sure?"

"I'm willing to find out."

He put his head down and stirred his spoon around some more. "You're worried I'll kill him, aren't you?"

"Yes," she said quietly.

"Maybe I'd be doing you a favor."

"Maybe."

"Maybe if he was dead, you'd be free. Maybe you could go someplace else and find a new man and start a new life. You're an attractive woman."

"I don't want him to die," she said.

"It's kind of funny when you think about it," he said.

"What is?"

"You and me. Sitting here."

"I guess it is, yes."

He looked at her. "I'm sorry he left you."

"And I'm sorry for you. You look pretty unhappy."

He shrugged. "I've never been a very happy man, anyway. Beth leaving just kind of fit right in with everything else."

"There's always the chance you're not as fast as you think you are."

"I suppose."

"There's always the chance that Frank might get lucky and kill you."

"Yes, I suppose there is that chance."

"Would she be worth dying for?"

He smiled sadly. "Apparently Frank thinks so."

She lowered her head. It was several long moments before he realized she was crying.

"I'm sorry," he said. "I shouldn't have made that smart remark. I was just feeling mean."

She shook her head. "It wasn't that. It's that I just finally realized you really are going to fight him."

"Probably."

"And there's nothing I can say or do to stop you."

"I want her back. I shouldn't, but I do."

"Maybe we should just both go away and leave them alone. Then there wouldn't be any need for a fight."

"He shouldn't have stolen her from me."

"Women aren't property. He didn't steal

her. She went because she wanted to go."

He reached across the table and touched her hand. "You're a nice woman, you know that?"

She was sniffling again. "Thank you."

"Maybe things'll work out. Maybe there won't be a fight."

"Do you really think so?" Her head came up so fast and she sounded so young and earnest that Rittenauer felt sad for her.

"It's possible," he said. "It's possible." Then, "Now, c'mon, and I'll walk you back to your hotel."

She smiled at him then, her first good true smile tonight; and he saw the beauty she'd once been and the beauty she still had in a certain worn and wan way.

"C'mon," he said, taking her hand and helping her from the booth.

Chapter Eight

Hollister, who had been born on a Kansas farm, had started what he called his "professional life" at the age of eighteen. He'd worked first as a gambler for a variety of saloons in a variety of backwater towns, and then as a saloon-keeper for a man dying of a heart ailment. The old man had given Hollister a cut of everything, including whiskey, cards, and girls. Soon enough Hollister was able to start buying the fancy clothes he had seen on his trips to Chicago and Kansas City. He was now twenty-three years old.

The following year he met Tom Adair, a man ten years older, and smarter and infinitely meaner. Hollister had once seen two bouncers work over a cardsharp in a back alley. He'd never forgotten the sounds the men's fists had made, or the way the cardsharp had mewled and bawled for mercy. Finally, when the cardsharp had begun puking up blood, Hollister had had to go back inside, unable to watch any more.

Adair was different. Adair exulted in violence of all kinds. He even treated business as a form of violence, becoming rich and powerful by exploiting the cattle market in mining boom towns.

In 1871 Adair had seen more than three hundred thousand head of stock move into the Plains States. He'd also seen how eagerly the beeves were snatched up by hungry customers. From then on, he was relentless about driving his cattle across the Plains to western markets. Mostly this was done by means of long trail drives rather than trains because he'd felt — before he'd become a railroad owner himself, that is — that trains cut into efficiency and dependability where shipping cattle was concerned. Plus, he considered railroad men to be the most ruthless and dishonest of all Yankee businessmen, especially since there was evidence that the railroads themselves were secretly working with stockyards and meatpacking plants to fix the price of beef. Gradually, however, as 1890 came and more than ten million head were moved out of the southwest alone, Adair came to see how valuable railroads could be in driving up consumer prices and keeping them there, thereby making rich cattlemen even richer. Cattlemen like himself.

Hollister had gone to work for Adair eight years ago. Within the first three months, he'd met two cabinet officers from the Harrison administration, several cattle ranchers rich enough to afford their own private railroad cars, and whores who had good teeth, well-bathed bodies, and genteel tongues, not the sort of whores he'd known previously.

He did not mind being a fetch-and-step man for Adair; Adair paid him well and treated him with a certain grudging respect. Where Adair was often loud and arrogant, putting people off with his demands, Hollister was more reasonable and generally got his way with people.

Hollister thought of all this as he shaved this morning, the sunlight golden and dusty in the hotel shaving mirror. Being just six o'clock, the town was not much alive yet, and would not be for another hour or so. Hollister, who didn't drink, was always up early. He believed that this helped account for his successful life. He was busy working when other men were still whining for their wives to give them morning sex.

Hollister did not much like women. Once a month he went to a whore house and chose a very young whore. Once upstairs and with virtually no conversation — the gold piece he put on the bureau as soon as he entered the room said quite enough — he fell to it. Sex for him was quick and impersonal. He did not like the way women smelled, or the way they felt after they reached a certain age, or the way they asked question after question.

He had been married once very briefly. By the end of the relationship he hadn't even been able to have sex with her any more. All she did was put on her pretty clothes and sit in front of the mirror and sob inconsolably. After she'd signed the necessary legal documents, he'd given her $3,000 in cash and told her to never contact him again.

He looked more closely at the face in the mirror now. He figured he was handsome, despite his extra weight, and he supposed that in his fancy suits he looked quite formidable. But his face had always amused him; it seemed to have nothing whatsoever to do with the being it hid. Where the face was open and ordinary, the man it hid was neither.

Bending to the basin, he washed the shaving soap off, washed under his arms, and splashed water on his chest and arms, drying off with a clean white nubby towel.

From there, he moved quickly, putting

on a clean white percale shirt and a clean collar. The suit he selected was gray, the cravat a deep red, almost wine-colored. He put a rag to his angular, Edwardian shoes. He liked them deep black and shiny.

The last item he put on his person was a small .44 that fit snugly into the waist of his trousers. While he often took target practice with Adair, he'd never had to use his gun in any sort of altercation. He hoped that his luck would continue.

"You didn't sleep again?" Beth asked, rolling over in bed and looking at Frank sitting on the bay window seat. He was smoking a cigarette. The smoke was blue in the morning light.

"No," he said, "I didn't." He sounded irritable.

Up and down the hall, you could hear the hotel coming alive — people clumping in shoes and slippers to the bathroom and back again.

"You're worried about something, aren't you?" she said.

He looked over at her and shook his head. "You bought that blouse yesterday, didn't you?"

"I —" Her first impulse was to lie. They'd had such an argument about it.

Finally, she'd promised that this once she wouldn't go behind his back and buy it. "Yes," she said. "Yes, I did."

"Beth, you know I don't have much money."

He sounded like a sulky little boy. She hated him when he sounded this way.

"It won't be long before we'll be touring again," she said, "and then we'll have plenty of money."

"Six months."

"What?"

"Six months before we start touring again. That's a long ways away. In the meantime —"

"In the meantime we'll be fine."

He swung his head around to look out the window again, sulky once more.

She took this opportunity to reach over and grab her robe off the chair next to the bed. She often, as last night, slept with no clothes on. The sight of her naked would make him passionate, and of late — with all his whining — she was less and less inclined to want sex with him. She wished they were back at the beginning of their time together. He'd been touring then and had plenty of money and absolutely no hesitation about spending it on her. She was not unsympathetic to Frank — indeed, knowing his money pressures, she felt quite sorry for him. But could you become passionate about a man you felt sorry for? Somehow she doubted it.

Getting out of bed and slipping quickly into her robe, she suddenly remembered the dream — nightmare, really — she'd had last night. About her neck. What had her mother told her? "Nothing tells more about a woman's age than her neck," she'd said. Beth shuddered, recalling the dream images now, the way her neck had been wattled and whorled with flesh and deep, deep lines. In the dream, she'd worn a succession of high, lacy collars so that nobody could see her neck. But then a very handsome and elegant man who had spent most of an evening at a fashionable party watching her across the room had suddenly become a brute. He'd stood in front of her and ripped away the lacy collar, seeing for himself what lay beneath. She'd screamed and slapped the man, but he had only laughed.

Now, as she walked over to Frank, she touched her neck, felt the soft flesh of it. Self-consciously she drew the collar of her robe up so that it covered as much of her throat as possible.

"Frank."

"What?"

"Let's have a nice day today."

He was still turned away from her, looking out the window.

"Why don't you give me some time to get dressed and then we can go downstairs and have some breakfast," she said. "Wouldn't you enjoy that?"

He looked back at her. Even his eyes looked sulky now. "I suppose."

She smiled. "Why don't you go for a walk? Maybe you'll be in a better mood."

She could see that he wanted to protest, but he finally gave up, went over and got his shirt and tugged it on. He jerked on his boots and pulled his trousers down over them. "How long will you need?"

"Maybe a half hour."

"All right."

He wouldn't look at her. Not meet her eye, anyway. "I really don't want to argue today, Frank."

"You think I do?"

And with that he left.

The main street was noisy with the chink of wagons, the laughter of children, and the general din of commerce. A water wagon went by, dousing the yellow dust that would otherwise be drifting up from the street; and ladies twirled parasols of a dozen different colors.

A woman noticed him. True, she was older and she was not what you'd call beautiful, but she *was* a woman and she *was* watching him. Already he felt better about himself and better about this day. The gaze of a woman could do that for him — make him feel special, powerful. Not even gold could quite equal the kick of a woman expressing interest in him.

When he reached the corner where the woman stood, he tipped his hat and smiled slyly, as if they shared some wonderful and special secret. He wished now he'd shaved and put on fresh clothes. The woman, obviously respectable and just as obviously married, smiled slyly right back.

He passed a tavern, and for a moment the smell of hops and malt appealed to him. But no, he did not want to be half-drunk today while Beth led him from one store to another or as they sat through their long lunch. He knew that they soon had to be kind to each other again or they would drift apart for sure.

It was money; always, it was money.

"Good morning."
"Good morning," Frank Evans replied. It was ten minutes later and he was circling

through the green city park. He had no idea who the man was who'd fallen into step with him.

"That's a nice bandstand over there."

"It sure is," Frank agreed.

"And a nice wading pool for the youngsters."

"Very nice."

"It's not the sort of day a fellow would want to work now, is it?"

"No, not at all."

"Get a good book and a blanket and stretch out and spend your time reading."

Frank didn't know how to read, but he did appreciate the pastoral scene the other man was painting for him.

"You're Frank Evans, aren't you?"

"Yes; yessir, I am."

"How many men do you suppose you've killed?"

So there you had it, what this man really wanted. Despite his fancy clothes, despite his somewhat sophisticated ways, he was no better than a punk kid who wanted to shine up to the gunslinger.

"Oh, it's too early in the day to talk about that."

"No, seriously now, how many do you suppose?"

Frank sighed. "The stories I keep hearing say twelve. But it's really eight."

"Eight," the man said, "my."

They were now at the east edge of the park. Babies in buggies were being pushed by pretty young mothers in long skirts and aprons. Five- and six-year-olds climbed trees and swings and chutey-chutes with the stealth of monkeys.

Frank stopped walking and asked, "You got a name?"

"Now don't go getting mad, Mr. Evans."

"You heard me. Your name."

"Hollister. Walter Hollister." Instead of offering his hand, the man put a small white business card in Frank's fingers.

Frank pretended to read the card. "What do you want with me?"

"Business."

"Business? What kind of business?"

"Very profitable business, Mr. Evans. At least potentially." Hollister pointed to the northern edge of the park. "Have you seen the zoo?"

"No."

"It's not much, just a camel and a fox and a very old lion, but why don't we go take a look? Give us someplace to walk to as we talk."

"I still want to know what kind of business you're talking about?" Frank didn't move.

Hollister looked right at him and said, "I'm going to give you a perfectly legal chance to kill Ben Rittenauer and collect ten thousand dollars cash for doing so."

"What the hell are you talking about, mister?"

"Let's walk over to the zoo and I'll tell you."

The camel was pathetic: scraggly and filthy and fly-bothered. He switched his tail like a horse.

Frank and Hollister stood looking at him inside his rope corral. He was ground-tied and obviously not going anywhere — poor bastard had neither the strength nor the gumption.

Hollister had explained it to Frank once and now Frank was having him go back through it again.

"You say it's legal?"

"Perfectly legal. There'll be a couple hundred witnesses to say it was a fair fight."

Lately, the closer the calendar got to the turn of the century, the harder the law was getting on gunfighters, charging them with murder.

"Plus you've got Tom Adair backing you up. Do you seriously suppose that any town marshal or judge is going to question Tom Adair?"

"I suppose not."

"And then there's the matter of ten thousand dollars cash."

The thought of such money almost made him giddy. For the entire year they'd been together, he'd been promising Beth to take her to Frisco. With that much money, he'd take her to a lot of other places, too. Their relationship could be what it had been at the beginning. She was a girl to have fun with, to be young with. All you needed to keep her happy was money.

"You talked to Rittenauer about this?"

"Not yet. But I will very soon. Mr. Adair would like the fight to be this evening."

Frank whistled. "That don't leave us much time."

"You're interested then, Mr. Evans?"

"Sure."

"Then I can count on you being at the Box Y?"

"If Rittenauer's there."

"I'll go talk to Rittenauer now and then get back with you."

"Fine."

Hollister smiled. "May I be honest, Mr. Evans?"

"Be my guest."

"I guess I figured you'd be the tough one to convince."

"Oh. How's that?"

"Well, you know Ben Rittenauer's reputation."

"I see. You're saying he's faster than me?"

"I'm saying that's his reputation. And you did sort of help yourself to his woman."

"You trying to get me to change my mind?"

"I just want you to be sure. I don't want to promise Mr. Adair something I can't deliver."

"If Rittenauer's there at five, I'll be there at five."

Hollister glanced over at the broken-down camel and shook his head. "Almost feel sorry for the old fellow, don't you?" Then he looked straight back at Frank and said, "He doesn't seem to know that his time has passed."

With that, Hollister left Frank alone in the park.

Chapter Nine

When Guild woke up in the morning, the first thing he thought about was his conversation with Hollister and Adair. Guild had said he wouldn't help them, but that didn't mean they couldn't help themselves. Hollister himself would probably go talk to the two gunfighters.

He ate Mrs. Tomlin's breakfast too quickly for any real appreciation of the trouble she'd taken with the eggs, bacon, and sliced potatoes. Then he spent his remaining time in the house apologizing for being in such a hurry.

"You look worried, Leo," Mrs. Tomlin said.

"I am worried," Guild said.

"Anything I can do?"

"I wish there was," Guild said.

The first place he went looking was the hotel where Frank Evans stayed. He asked the clerk, "You seen Evans this morning?"

" 'Bout half an hour ago."

"Oh?"

The clerk nodded at the door, its windows filled with golden dusty sunshine. "Believe he said he was going for a walk."

The town wasn't that big, Guild reasoned. He shouldn't have that tough a time finding Evans. Maybe in the meantime he'd run into Ben Rittenauer and have a chance to talk to at least one of them.

He walked up and down ten blocks of board sidewalk and down dusty alleys. He walked along the river through the park.

No sign of Evans or Rittenauer. But he kept looking anyway.

After leaving Hollister, Frank Evans was as exultant as a kid on his birthday. He went to the barber, where he got a good hot shave and his hair slicked down. In the back room were tubs where you could bathe for fifteen cents, so he got himself a good hot bath, too.

He hated to put on the same dirty clothes, so he sent the black man who worked the tubs for new clothes down the street. He'd have to trust the man's tastes, but how wrong could you go with a white percale shirt and dark trousers? In the meantime, he splashed rose-smelling after-shave on himself.

Frank Evans hadn't spent any money on himself in two months. Cash was so low, he'd been afraid to. Anyway, Beth spent enough money for the both of them. But now that he was actually laying out cash for himself, he felt almost dizzy with pleasure. He felt like his old self again, the tent-show self, the one who swaggered around playing the grim gunfighter to the awed rubes. This self spent as much money on himself as he chose.

The black man was back in fifteen minutes. He'd done a good job choosing clothes, so Frank tipped him a quarter. The man thanked him five times.

After he left the barbershop, smelling and looking brand-new, Frank headed down the street to where a plump Slavic woman was selling flowers. He bought a half-dozen roses, pricking himself on one of the thorns. Then he went back to his hotel.

Ten thousand dollars. It was all he could think of. Ten thousand dollars. No more dreading that Beth would sneak off and find another man. She'd never leave him when he had ten thousand dollars.

He eased open the door and went inside.

She sat at the dressing table combing her beautiful red hair. She wore only a silk undergarment that enhanced the full breasts she was so proud of.

She glanced up at him in the mirror. She was startled by what she saw. He'd left unshaven and rumpled and returned slicked up, wearing different clothes, and bearing flowers.

He went straight over to her and kissed her on the forehead and then grandly presented her with the roses.

She cradled the wrapped flowers as if they were a precious infant and said, "You seem to be celebrating, Frank."

"I am."

"New clothes and a shave and —"

"By tomorrow morning, we're going to have ten thousand dollars cash."

He had never seen her look happier or more radiant. The mention of ten thousand dollars put a grin on her face that was wonderful to see. "Ten thousand dollars? But how?"

"Just to do a little shooting is all," Frank said.

"For a show of some kind?"

For the first time, he was hesitant. "No, not a show exactly."

He walked over to the window. The main street was alive. He wanted to be down there fancied up this way, people staring at him and knowing who he was.

Not facing her, he said, "Ben Rittenauer and I are going to have a gunfight."

"Frank, are you kidding?"

She set the flowers down and came over to him. Touched his elbow. He still wouldn't look at her.

"Frank, I asked you if you were kidding."

"No, I'm not kidding."

"But Frank, you're no match for Ben, and you know it."

Now he looked at her. "He's not who he used to be. He's getting older."

"But so are you."

He took her arms and pulled her to him. He hugged her. "Just think of all the things we can do with that money."

"But Frank —"

"Ten thousand dollars, Beth. We'll go to Chicago and Kansas City and —"

"Oh, Frank," she said, as if she were talking to a little boy with too many fanciful notions. "Oh, Frank."

And then they just stood there a long time, not speaking, Frank thinking of the ten thousand dollars and her thinking how Frank would soon be dead and it would be time to find another man.

Guild found the two of them — Ben

Rittenauer and Hollister — in a restaurant. They sat at a table along the wall. Coffee and bacon smelled good on the morning air.

Hollister saw Guild before Rittenauer did; he frowned.

Guild went over anyway and said, "I wouldn't have anything to do with him, Rittenauer."

Rittenauer looked amused by this. "You wouldn't, huh? And just who the hell are you?"

Hollister said, "His name is Leo Guild. Frank Evans took his wife away from him."

"Oh, that's right, Guild," Rittenauer said. He smiled a hard quick smile. "I guess that gives us something in common, losing women to Evans."

"Hollister and his boss don't give a damn whether you live or die. They just want a show put on so all their rich friends can have a laugh."

"Maybe you should have been a preacher, Guild," Hollister said.

"Maybe I should have."

"I don't remember inviting you over, Guild. Why don't you go find a table of your own?" Hollister said. He nodded at Rittenauer. "Ben and I were having a nice pleasant talk over a nice pleasant breakfast. Right, Ben?"

86

Rittenauer looked up at Guild. "That's the truth, Guild."

"Maybe Evans won't do it," Guild said. "Maybe he'll be sensible for once."

"Afraid you're a little late for that," Hollister said. "I've already talked to Evans and he's delighted with the opportunity."

Guild said, "You know damn well Evans doesn't have a chance against Rittenauer here."

Hollister shrugged. "That's the thing about gunfights. There's always a surprise or two. You never quite know for sure who's going to win."

Guild said to Rittenauer, "I suppose you've been waiting a long time for this."

"A long time," Rittenauer said. He studied Guild's calm face. "You mean you never thought of killing him yourself?"

"I thought about it."

"He's a little too free with other men's women."

"You make it sound as if the women don't play any part in this. They make choices the same as men do."

Rittenauer's face tightened. "I spent a lot of nights thinking about her in his bed. That's not a way to live."

"What makes you think she'll come back

to you even if you do kill him?"

Rittenauer grimaced. "Ten thousand dollars, Guild. That's what'll make her come back."

"And you'd want her back knowing that?"

"Hollister here was right, Guild. Maybe you should have been a preacher. Anyway, why the hell do you want to save his neck? You should be hoping I put two good bullets in his chest."

"You don't understand Guild here, Ben," Hollister said. "He's the noble sort. He's trying to do something nice for his ex-wife." He smiled. "The one Frank Evans took from him."

The waitress came to fill their cups again. Guild left.

The word had spread quickly and widely. Guild stopped into another restaurant down the street for a cup of coffee and a cigarette; and he heard four men at the counter discussing the impending gunfight. They sounded like children — eager, naive, bloodthirsty. In their minds neither Evans nor Rittenauer were human beings — they were some kind of mythical beings who did not have fears or hopes or come down with whooping cough or feel good on sunny days. They were just "gun-fighters," players in a play, and they did not have families who would mourn the loser or doll-like women who would exploit the winner. All the talk disgusted Guild. These men would never have nerve enough to get into a gunfight themselves, but they were eager enough to let someone else do it in their stead.

Guild left a nickel for his coffee and wandered back out into the street.

The sheriff, whose name was Carter, had a noble face. With his ringlets of gray hair, his Roman senator profile, and his deep, thunderous speaking voice, it was easy to see why he was serving his sixth term as the county's leading lawman. The only troubling aspect of Carter's whole show was his gaze. There was no mercy in his eyes, nor amusement. Maybe his job had made him this way, or maybe he'd always been this way and took the job because it encouraged his particular kind of coldness.

"Yes, I've heard about the gunfight, Guild." Carter shrugged. "I'm afraid I can't get excited about it."

"The state legislature passed two bills about gunfighting last year."

"That they did." The two men sat in a

small office with a large window and a nice big mahogany rolltop desk. Carter had set his big fine-tooled cowboy boots on the open desk. He sipped coffee after giving Guild his coffee.

"So what they're doing is illegal."

"I've got three deputies."

"All right. You've got three deputies."

"If I was to post them out at the Adair ranch, what the hell would I do about the rest of the county?"

"You don't need to post them. Just go to Adair now and tell him what you've heard and make clear that you plan to press charges if the gunfight takes place."

Carter laughed. "Yeah, and I'm sure old Tom would pay a lot of attention to me." Carter downed some more coffee. "He'd just smile and say 'Aw, hell, Carter, don't you have anything better to do than pick on rich old boys like myself?'" Carter shook his head. "It'd be good for my ego and my reputation to interfere with the gunfight — show people I can stand up to Tom Adair, after all — but to tell you the truth, no matter what I do, that gunfight is going to take place. At least if that's what Tom Adair wants. And there's nothing you can do or I can do to stop it."

"Evans is going to get killed."

"You won't find me shedding any tears over a gunny, I'm afraid."

Guild drained his coffee. "The only thing I can do is convince Evans he's going to get killed."

"Ten thousand dollars will make a man awful foolish and Adair knows it." He offered Guild a look at his Roman profile. He looked just the way he did on his RE-ELECT SHERIFF CARTER posters out in the front office, hammy as a Chautauqua Shakespearean. "Awful foolish."

Guild stood up. Carter wasn't a bad man or even a lazy one. Just realistic. There was little the law — any sort of law — could do to a man like Tom Adair.

Carter put out his hand and Guild shook it. "I'd like to see Tom Adair get his ass kicked around the block, Guild. If you can manage to pull it off, there'll be a special place in heaven for you."

Guild smiled. "I'm not sure heaven is the direction I'm headed, Sheriff."

Carter laughed. "We're probably headed in pretty much the same direction, Guild. Good luck with everything."

Chapter Ten

Sarah was sitting in a restaurant, sipping her morning coffee, when she heard the news about the gunfight.

A feeling of sickness spread from her stomach up to her chest and then down through her arms. The pace of her breathing increased, and she knew that soon she'd have a headache. She had felt this way the morning she'd heard that a plow horse had killed her youngest brother. This was a place beyond words or tears.

She realized now that she had always believed that Frank would come back to her, just as he'd always done before. He got tired of them, these women; or they got tired of him. He was winsome and darling, but nobody could be winsome or darling for long. They always found some subtle way of ending the relationship that allowed Frank to keep his considerable vanity and pride. And then he'd be back, full of hot promises and iron resolve. For a time she'd give him no solace, but then always, always she'd take him to her — as much his mother as his lover it sometimes seemed — and he would tell her all his fears and would love him all the more for these moments of honesty, the few moments when Frank faced the facts about himself, that he was getting older, that he was losing his skills as a gunfighter, and that much of the time he was frightened that somebody from his past, some punk who'd finally gotten good enough, would reappear and kill him. And they would lie in the darkness then and she would soothe him and then they would make soft, gentle love. He would whisper forgive me, forgive me and she would forgive him and forgive herself, too, for being so foolish where he was concerned, for without him she had no life. No life at all.

"Little more coffee?" the waitress asked, tilting her tin pot to Sarah's cup.

"No, thanks."

The waitress watched her carefully. "Are you all right?"

"Yes."

"You looked flushed. Like you might be feeling faint."

The waitress was gray-haired and maternal; Sarah appreciated her concern. "I'm fine, really."

"Whatever it is, I'm sure it'll work out."

Sarah smiled, knowing that tears stood in her eyes. "I sure hope it will, anyway."

She had no idea where to go, what to do, who to see. So she just walked, the way she always did in the first days of being left by Frank.

She went everywhere and nowhere, saw everything and nothing. An image of pink summer flowers and the scent of apple blossoms; a man shoveling fly-buzzed manure out of the livery; a young girl in a fluttery white dress leading a group of smaller children in ring-around-the-rosy; the chug and chuff of a steam engine as it gained purpose and power and headed east down tracks shining with sunlight. A plump priest in black cassock stood on the steps of his stone parish; on impulse — she was, after all, a Presbyterian — she went over and touched the hands he had folded on the rim of his girth. "Pray for me, Father," she said, but was gone before he could respond.

When she got back to her hotel, she saw Guild sitting in a leather chair in the lobby. He was smoking a cigarette and reading the newspaper. She hated to think it, but he looked old and sad in the way of the other old men who sat idly in the lobby.

He saw her over the top of his paper. He folded the paper neatly, put it down, and came over to her.

"Why don't we go for a walk?"

"Leo, I've been walking for the last hour. I'm tired of walking."

"Go out on the sidewalk, anyway. It's too quiet in here to talk."

As it was. All the old men were straining forward to hear what they were about to say.

She sighed. When Leo wanted you to do something, you usually did it.

She went out into the sunlight and stood on the sidewalk. People flowed by and jostled her. The air smelled of sunlight. She'd always thought that peculiar, that sunlight should have a scent.

Leo studied her with his blue, blue eyes and said, "I'm on my way over to the depot to buy you a ticket."

"What?"

"Just what I said. And I don't want no goddamned argument about it, do you understand?"

"But Leo —"

"You know what he's gone and done, with the gunfight and all, and you know

95

what the result is going to be. I don't want you around for it. You've had heartbreak enough with that tinhorn son of a bitch."

As she was often mother to Frank, so had Leo often been father to her. He was father now. Touched, she reached out a soft hand to his cheek. "I talked with Ben Rittenauer last night," she said.

"Oh?"

"He seems like a reasonable man."

"Meaning what?"

"Meaning I think I can talk him out of it."

"I don't think you know how much he hates Frank. Rittenauer has his pride like everybody else. And he's awful happy about that ten-thousand-dollar paycheck."

She smiled. "I still think I can talk him out of it, Leo."

"C'mon," he said, and took her by the elbow. He'd never been rough before. He was rough now.

"No, Leo, I don't want to go get a train ticket."

"Right now I don't give a damn what you want."

"No," she said.

He redoubled his grip on her elbow and tried tugging her in the direction of the depot.

People were gawking at them. How people loved the grief of strangers.

"No," she said again.

And then, with her free hand, she slapped him.

She knew instantly what she'd done. She had slapped not Leo, but Frank; all the years of loss and fear and shame, all those years boiling up suddenly and erupting as a slap on Leo's face.

"I'm sorry," she said.

She saw that he did not understand, that he was hurt and angry now. "Leo, I know you were only trying to help but —"

And then he was gone, the crowd claiming him. She couldn't even see his white hair now.

"Leo," she said to herself, realizing that she might have lost her last and best friend. "Leo."

She went upstairs and laid down, trying to sleep, but it didn't work. She went over to the window and looked out. She wanted suddenly to be out of this town. Forever. Maybe Leo was right, after all. Maybe the best thing was to get on a train and say goodbye to everything. For a long, bright moment she was filled with ridiculous joy. That was it. She'd leave town and start life afresh, make new friends, be her old happy self again, the self she'd been before Frank, before Leo even. The girl in her was what she'd lost somewhere, and it was the girl in her she wanted to find again.

But it ended, the hope, and she became aware of her fluttering heartbeat and the sticky anxious sweat on her arms, the dry panic in her throat. Frank. She could never leave him. Suddenly she had purpose again. She had to go see Ben Rittenauer before it was too late.

She came, as he knew she'd come, just as she had the other times she'd left him.

There always came the day when her knuckles would rap softly on the door, and she would say, in as sweet and soft a voice as she could possibly summon, "Ben. Ben, it's me."

And being the fool he was, Ben Rittenauer always opened the door to her.

As he did now.

"Hello, Ben."

"Hello."

"You're surprised to see me."

"No, no, I'm not, Beth."

She smiled. "Then at least glad to see me?"

"I'm not sure yet."

She gave him her little girl look. She was a past master at that little girl look. "It's awfully dark out here in this hallway."

"You'll survive."

"You won't let me in?"

"They don't like it when men have ladies in their rooms here."

"That never stopped you before."

"You never left me for Frank Evans before."

"People make mistakes."

"You've made more than your share."

"What if I say I'm sorry?"

He sighed. "Spare me that, anyway."

Her gaze got tougher. She hated it when her wiles didn't work. That's what she was all about, her wiles. "It is sort of ungallant for you to leave me out in the hall."

"I suppose it is," he said. And he walked into the room, letting her follow him in and close the door herself.

He stood for a moment in the middle of a long bar of dusty sunlight, then turned around. "You look good, I'll say that for you."

"You look good, too."

He smirked. "Sure I do, Beth."

She disregarded his implication that her flattery might be nothing more than another example of her wiles.

She looked around the room. "Not very festive, is it?"

"I haven't been in a festive mood lately."

She walked over to the cheap, chipped bureau and ran a white-gloved finger over the top. "They don't dust very often."

"I hadn't noticed."

She turned from the bureau and stared at him. "You need a woman, Ben."

He shrugged. "Maybe."

"I don't think I should have left you, Ben. I think I made a mistake."

He laughed. "So you did hear about it. I was wondering."

"Hear about what?"

"The gunfight. And the ten thousand dollars."

"That isn't the reason I'm here."

"Oh, no. It couldn't be. An honorable woman like you."

"You can sneer if you want to. But I really have missed you." She paused. "Haven't you missed me, Ben?"

For the first time he let his real anger show. "You know I have. But what the hell does that prove? I missed you the other times you walked out on me, too. That didn't mean you changed when you came back."

"I didn't know myself, Ben. Didn't

know what I truly wanted."

"And now you do?"

She nodded. "Now I do, Ben. I really do."

He walked over to the window and looked down into the dusty street. "I'm going to kill him," he said. "You know that, don't you?"

She said nothing.

"You know that, don't you?" he asked again.

And finally she said it. "Yes, Ben. I know."

He came away from the window then, back to where she stood in the middle of the room.

He took her in his arms and kissed her.

Chapter Eleven

Sarah was ten feet from Ben Rittenauer's door when it opened and Beth came out.

"I'll see you later, then," Beth said. She paused in the doorway long enough to kiss him full on the mouth. She turned around, pulling the door shut behind her, and started down the hall. Then she saw Sarah.

At first, Beth looked as though she were going to say something harsh, but finally she just pulled herself up tall and pushed past Sarah, as if the woman weren't worth speaking to. In a rustle of organdy, Beth disappeared down the second-floor steps.

Sarah hurried to Ben Rittenauer's door and knocked. Having seen Beth here — and easily surmising what had happened — Sarah felt more certain than ever that she could convince the gunfighter to withdraw from the fight this evening.

Ben Rittenauer did not look happy to see her. "I was trying to take a nap."

"I won't take much of your time."

The brief friendliness they'd enjoyed the

other night was gone. This was the hard, cold Ben Rittenauer of gunfighter legend.

He sighed. "C'mon in. But I really want you to make it short."

Once she was inside, Sarah said, "I saw her leaving your room. Beth, I mean. You're going back with her, aren't you?"

He glared at her. "Seems like that would be my business, wouldn't it?"

"I didn't mean anything by that. I just —"

"Why'd you come up here, anyway?"

Sarah started chewing on the inside of her lip. She did this so fervently sometimes that she drew blood. "So I could talk you out of fighting Frank. But now I don't have to."

"Oh? And how would that be?"

She was almost exultant. "You've got her back. Now there's no reason to fight him."

"That's how it works, huh? I've got her back and that's all I care about?"

"Why, yes. What else would you want?"

She could see how angry he was. "What about my pride?" He hesitated. "And what about the money?"

"Is money really all that important to you? Enough to risk —"

He shook his head. "You know something?" He sounded warmer suddenly, more the way he'd been the other night, and she was surprised by this.

"What?"

"You're a good woman."

"Oh." She blushed. "Thanks."

"You think I'm just saying that but I'm not. You really are good. True and honest and loyal."

She shook her head. "I left my first husband a long time ago. I'm not the saint you seem to be saying."

"But after that you changed. You became a good woman." He sighed. He looked sad now instead of angry, and there seemed to be a weariness behind his words. "Frank and Beth and me — we're riffraff, Sarah. You don't seem to understand that. We don't have a good or true bone in our bodies." He came over and took her hand. "You deserve better than Frank, Sarah." He looked at her and smiled. "You ever thought of going back to Guild?"

"Not after what I did to him. It could never be the same."

"He's a good man, Sarah."

"I know he is."

"Sarah, I want that money."

She started crying. "Oh, God, Mr. Rittenauer. Does it really have to be that way?"

"I'm afraid it does."

"But you'll kill him."

"If I'm lucky, I will. If he's lucky, he'll kill me."

"You're willing to take that chance?"

"For ten thousand dollars I am."

"Oh, God, Mr. Rittenauer," she said again and started crying all the harder.

He came over to her and took her in his arms, holding her with great, almost reverent delicacy. He sort of started rocking her then, a barely perceptible movement, the kind of subtle thing you do instinctively when you hold a small child.

"You know what you should do, Sarah," he said softly. "You should go over to that depot and buy yourself a ticket to the farthest place you can go on this continent, and then get on that train and never think about any one of us again."

Crying into his shoulder, she said, "That's what Leo says I should do."

"Leo's a smart man."

"Oh, God, Mr. Rittenauer, do you really have to fight him?"

"Yes," he said, in that strange soft voice again, "yes, Sarah, I'm afraid I do."

"And I can't change your mind?"

He took her by the shoulders and held her out from him so he could see her face. "You do what I tell you."

"About the train?"

"Yes. About the train. As far and as fast as you can get away from the three of us. Somewhere out there is a good man who'll appreciate you."

"But, Mr. Rittenauer, won't you —"

He shook his head. "You won't change my mind, Sarah, no matter what you say. I want and I need that money, and I plan to get it. Or at least I plan to try. I'm sorry. That's just how it is."

Finally, feeling exhausted, she realized that Ben Rittenauer was not in fact going to change his mind. He was going to go through with the gunfight.

"All right, then," she said. "All right."

In a moment, she was just faint footsteps down the hall.

Guild saw her leaving Rittenauer's hotel. He'd been looking for her the past hour.

He fell into step with her. "How're you doing?"

"I didn't mean to slap you."

"I know. You just kind of startled me is all."

"Ben Rittenauer thinks you're a fine man."

"He must be running for office and wanting my vote."

"You always did have a crazy sense of humor."

But he noticed that she didn't laugh. She was scarcely hearing anything he said.

"I really am sorry about slapping you, Leo," she said.

"I know. It's all right." There was a restaurant on their left. "How about some coffee?"

"I don't know what I'm going to do about Frank, Leo."

Now, she wasn't listening at all. He steered her into the restaurant. She went along like a docile child.

It was after the lunch rush, and the place was empty except for an old-timer in the back reading a magazine and chewing on a cigar stub that looked to be near as old as he was.

Guild went up to the counter and got them two cups of coffee and brought them back.

She had her face in her hands and was shaking her head as if demons were whispering filthy words to her. The Greek café owner was watching her with lurid fascination. She was offering him a little something to break up the otherwise dull day.

She parted her hands, looked at Guild, and smiled. "You really are a fine man, Leo."

"And here I keep trying not to get a swelled head."

"Would you talk to him for me, Leo?"

"To Frank?"

She nodded.

Guild sighed. "Why do you think he'll listen to me?"

"You two may not be the best of friends, but he respects your judgment. Maybe you can make him see that Ben Rittenauer will kill him."

"He doesn't know that?"

"Maybe he knows it, but he won't admit it to himself." She sipped her coffee. "Besides, there isn't anything to fight over anymore anyway."

"No?"

"No." Then she told him about Beth going up to Rittenauer's room. "Obviously, she figures Ben is going to win, so she wants to be there when he gets the ten thousand dollars."

"Nice woman."

"Ben says none of them are nice, him or Frank or her. He thinks you and I should get back together."

"He does, huh?"

"You're blushing."

"Thanks for pointing that out."

"I guess I shouldn't have said that."

"It's all right. There was a lot of years when I thought that would still be a good idea."

"Us getting back together?"

"Yes."

"It wouldn't work, Leo."

"I know. But it's nice to think about sometimes."

She hesitated. "Will you see him, Leo?"

"If you want me to."

"I'd really appreciate it."

"He up in his room?"

"He should be."

"Guess I'll go over there then."

She reached out a hand and touched his. There were calluses on her hands, and the flesh was tough from hard work. Which figured. She would have done all the chores, all the hardscrabble tasks. Frank Evans was only interested in glory.

Guild stood up. "You wait here."

At the Adair ranch, two Mexican laborers were putting up the last of the bunting on the bandstand. One thought to himself that even on an ordinary day, a day with no festivities, the Adair ranch was a beautiful spread. The home itself was a vast Victorian, with gaslights out front and stable room for three surreys that were as smart as any you'd see in Juarez. Governors had many times stayed here, as had senators and even a stage star or two, including Miriam Reynolds herself.

Despite the endless hours it took to get ready for an occasion, the men felt a real pride in dressing the place up. With a hundred fancy guests and a ten-piece band playing Sousa marches in the early part of the evening and Stephen Foster later, the ranch became something more than a mere ranch. From trains, from stagecoaches, from surreys they came, men in top hats and brocaded vests and women in picture hats and sneers for the help. They would be waited on for the next twenty-four hours by black men and yellow men and red men "broken and tamed," as Tom Adair always put it, by his power and his money.

Despite the work involved, despite the backbreaking labor, there was, too, the curious exhilaration of standing so close to such festivities — the glowing paper lanterns against the dark prairie sky, the spectacle of so many beautiful women being whirled around the makeshift dance floor. And then there were all the things one could steal, the food and liquor and tinkling coins dropped drunkenly by the swaggering male guests.

And this year there was one more thing: a gunfight. The men had never sensed such excitement on the ranch before. Two bona fide gunfighters in a bona fide gunfight. Right here on the ranch. Tonight.

The gringos were a strange and selfish and savage people, the Mexican thought. But one thing you had to say for them. They knew how to put on a party.

Who but a gringo would think of having two men try to kill each other for the pleasure and amusement of an audience?

Only a gringo, the Mexican thought, going back to finish off the bunting. Only a gringo.

Chapter Twelve

Guild wanted to stand in the hallway sunlight, lazy as a cat. He wished he'd never
heard of any of them so his mind could be
free as his body lazed in the golden dusty
warmth of the sunbeams. But he was getting old, and memory was a burden — all
those regrets, all those foolishnesses, the
good people seeming to recede more and
more, the bad people remaining as vivid as
ever. He wished there were some way to
take a knife and just cut all memory away,
like a cancer of some sort. But only the
grave and the darkness beyond could do
that. Anyway he'd made Sarah a promise,
so now he raised his fist and slammed it
against the door. When it finally opened it
wasn't Frank Evans who answered, it was
Beth.

The first thing he noticed, of course, was
her black eye. It had swelled the flesh
around her right eye and looked to be fresh
and painful.

All his worked-up anger went. Much as

he disliked the woman, he didn't like to see her this way. He hated men who knocked women around.

"Afternoon," he said, cordial as he could be.

"What is it you want, Mr. Guild?"

"I'd like to see Frank."

"He isn't here."

"I see."

She stared hard at him. "Don't you just love big strong men who push women around?"

"He find out you went over to see Rittenauer?"

"Yes."

She opened the door wider. He could see into the room now. A large traveling bag was sitting on the bed; she had been in the process of packing.

"Ben never hit me," she said. "Not once in eight years. No matter how bad things got." Her lower lip was quivering. She'd be better off to cry and just get it over with. "Ben'll be very mad when he sees my eye."

Guild said, "You could stop it."

"I beg your pardon?"

"The fight. You could stop it. You could pack up and take Rittenauer and leave town."

"And why would I do that?"

Guild said, "I assume you're going back to Rittenauer because you love him. Seems to me you'd want to protect the man you love."

"It isn't Ben who needs protecting. It's Frank. Anyway, they both want the money. Neither one of them's ever had a chance for money like this."

"To amuse robber barons," Guild said and shook his head. "Maybe that's the biggest pity of all. The crowd who'll be watching."

She seemed bored now, hurried. "I need to go back to my packing. You'll likely find Frank in the saloon downstairs."

She closed the door.

Frank Evans was indeed downstairs. He stood at the far end of the bar, alone. He wore a clean boiled white shirt and dark trousers. His Texas hat was off and sitting on the bar. He looked handsome as ever but faded, too, somehow. Behind him many of the customers whispered and pointed to him. The pending gunfight this afternoon had made him a celebrity again. Given his ego, he should have been happy. He looked miserable.

Guild walked over to him. "Sarah wants me to talk you out of fighting Rittenauer."

In front of Frank was a shell and a shot. He had touched neither one. "She does, huh?"

"She's still in love with you."

"She tell you to say that?"

"No. Unfortunately it's something I figured out all by myself."

"Still don't like me, huh?"

"Not much."

"Then you should be happy I'm fighting Rittenauer. From all that buzzing I get, Rittenauer's supposed to beat me without much trouble."

"She wants you two to get out of here and try it again. This time she wants you to be faithful; she wants you to take up farming or something like that."

"Can you ever see me doing that?"

"Guess not."

"Then why talk about it?"

"Because you owe her."

"The hell. She's free, white, and twenty-one."

"She's also stuck by you all these years."

"I never said it would be easy."

"He'll kill you," Guild said.

"So I'm told."

"So the ten thousand will be moot. Where you're going, it won't matter."

For a moment Guild thought he heard

tears in Frank Evans' voice. "That bitch Beth went to see him."

"I know."

"Behind my goddamn back. Like some whore. And you know why she did it?"

Guild said nothing.

"Because of the goddamned money. The goddamned money. Can you believe that?"

"Rittenauer thinks you three are pretty lousy people. He wants Sarah to get on a train, go far away, and forget she ever knew the three of you. Seems he cares more about her than you do."

But Frank Evans wasn't listening. He was staring off into space, saying, "Can you imagine that bitch's face when I kill Rittenauer? She's going to be goddamned sorry she ever went to see him, let me tell you that."

He made a fist and brought it down hard on the bar.

Behind him, a hush had fallen. All the customers — afraid and excited in equal parts now — watched him carefully. Maybe he'd do something here that they could talk about for long years in the future.

"That bitch is going to be sorry," Frank Evans said. "Let me tell you that."

Guild watched Evans carefully. He felt

sorry for the man he'd hated so long. He remembered his own bitterness when Sarah had left him for Frank — it was a form of madness, actually, what you went through when a woman left you like that — and he hated to see even Frank Evans go through it.

"Why don't you let me take those from you?" Guild nodded to the shot and the shell.

Frank Evans smiled. "Don't worry, pally. I'd never take a drink before a gun-fight. I've just got these here to have something to look at." He turned around and glared at the customers watching him. "I sure as hell don't want to look at all the punks and nellies just waiting to see me get killed."

They averted their eyes, bowed their heads, and began muttering through sudden conversations.

Frank Evans turned back to Guild. "That's the worst of it, you know."

"The onlookers?"

"Absolutely. Just waiting for you to die."

"You didn't need to hit her," Guild said.

"I'd say that's my business."

"Words would have been sufficient."

"She's a bitch."

"I'm not denying that. But she's also a

woman. I don't put much store in men who hit women."

"Noble son of a bitch, aren't you?"

Frank Evans was getting mean now. Guild was sick of him. "Anything you want me to tell Sarah?"

"Tell her I think it's a good idea."

"What is?"

"Ben's notion that she should get on a train and get away from the three of us as fast as she can."

"Anything else I should tell her?"

They stared at each other. Obviously Guild was hoping for some warm, sentimental words to take back to her.

Frank Evans said, "Why don't you get the hell out of here and leave me alone, Leo?"

"Good afternoon, ma'am."

"Afternoon."

"Help you with something?"

"Looking for a gun, I guess."

"Got anything particular in mind?"

"Just thought you could show me some things."

"Be glad to."

"I don't want to spend a fortune."

"That narrows it down some right there."

The clerk, a little bald man in a dusty white apron that rode his paunch, showed Sarah over to two glass display cases filled with guns.

Sight of all the armaments disgusted her. Even though she'd grown up on a farm with a father and two brothers who'd hunted, she always hated guns: the noise they made, the stink of them just after they were fired, and the destruction they brought — beautiful pheasants tumbling from the sky, or a white-spotted fawn collapsing to stain the green grass with her red blood.

"What's that one?"

"Colt. Colt Peacemaker."

"May I see it?"

"Of course."

For a moment, she closed her eyes and gave herself over to the smells of the general store, the scent of mustard seeds and sweet hair tonic, the smells of baking soda and winesap apples, the odor of tobacco and coffee beans. She remembered these smells from her girlhood days, when her father had brought the kids to town in the clattery wagon. How easy things had been when she was a girl. How easy.

"You know how to shoot?"

"A little bit."

"Well, here, then, why don't you hold it."

So she took it and held it. Sighted along it the way her father had always taught her. Pulled back the trigger. Pretended she was firing.

"How do you like it?"

"Seems all right."

"Nice price on it." He told her the price.

"Isn't that expensive?"

"No, ma'am. No, ma'am, not at all."

She sighted along it again. "Well," she said.

"Got some bullets I'll throw in, too. Half box of them."

He was selling her. She hated to be sold.

"All right, then. Oh, wait a second."

"Ma'am?"

"I just want to see if this will fit in my purse."

"Oh."

She smiled. "I don't want to go walking around with a gun in my hand."

"No, I guess not." For the first time, the man looked at her carefully. He seemed somewhat disturbed by what he saw in her eyes.

She slipped the Colt in her purse. "There," she said. "Fits perfectly."

"Kinda thought it might." He sounded relaxed, but he was still watching her eyes carefully.

They went to the front of the store. The smells were even stronger up here. They were like heady perfume, and she almost swooned. She could hear her father's clattery wagon and feel her brother Tom's bony elbow as they pushed and jostled each other on the way into town. She wondered what Tom was doing this very second. She'd like to talk to him. Perhaps he could talk her out of what she had in mind.

"You said the bullets were free?"

He picked up a small greasy box and rattled the bullets inside. "These leftovers are free. If you want a whole box, I'll have to charge you."

"I'm sure those will be fine."

He wrote her up a ticket. "You've got the gun in your purse?"

"Yes."

"You want me to wipe it down for you or anything?"

"It'll be fine."

He stared at her again. "You feeling all right, ma'am?"

"I'm fine. Why do you ask?"

"You look a little peaked is all."

"No, I'm fine. Really."

He nodded to her purse. "You know I could always hold on to that for you."

"Sir?"

"In case today isn't a good day to buy a gun, I mean. Maybe it's something you'd want to think over a little longer and come back tomorrow or the next day."

She stared right back at him. "No, today's a fine day to buy a gun."

"Whatever you say, ma'am," he said, and finished writing her ticket.

Just as she was going out the door, she paused on the threshold to breathe in one last smell of the place. She could hear her mother exclaiming over the fresh coffee beans and lifting blue taffeta to press gently to her cheek. Her mother had been so pretty.

Then she went out into the dust and heat and horseshit of the street.

Sheriff Carter was finishing his third cup of coffee of the afternoon when Cletus Baines, the clerk at the general store, came rushing into his office.

Cletus was way overweight these days — his wife baked a good cherry pie. Plus Cletus, sorry to say, was one lazy son of a bitch.

"Got one for you," he panted.

"Got 'one' what, Cletus?"

"You know. Suspicious person buying a firearm."

"Oh. Right."

They'd made their pact so long ago —
years ago — that Carter had forgotten
about it. "First off, Cletus, why don't you
catch your breath?"

The little fat man stood there sweaty and
red-faced, virtually gasping for air. He had
to lose some weight. Had to.

"Woman," he said when his breathing
was less ragged.

"Woman?"

"Woman bought the Colt."

"I see. Know who she was?"

"Think she's got something to do with
Ben Rittenauer."

"She's quite a looker, isn't she."

"Not that one. The other one."

Cletus Baines described his customer.
Carter recognized her immediately.

"Funny," he said.

"Huh?" Cletus said, at last getting his
breath under control again.

"Why she'd buy a gun."

"She acted funny, too."

"How so?"

"Nervous and kind of — I don't know
how to describe it — agitated, I guess."

Carter was up on his feet and reaching
for the big white hat that flattered his
Roman profile. He hated trouble in town.
Trouble always had a way of making the

sheriff look bad — as if he could not keep it in check, as if chaos squatted like an invading army on the edge of town — so he was grateful that Cletus had come over.

"I owe you a couple of schooners, Cletus," he said as he escorted the man out. To a deputy showing an Indian prisoner how he wanted the floor scrubbed, Carter said, "I'm going to go hunt up Leo Guild. You hold down the fort for me, all right?"

The deputy nodded.

Carter and Cletus went out into the sunlight. Cletus didn't have a hat, and he blinked against the hot yellow rays.

"Maybe I'll stop by the pharmacy and have Biner fix me one of his vanilla shakes," he said.

He was asking Carter's permission, wanting the big, trim man to say it was okay to go on indulging himself.

Carter cracked him hard across the rim of his paunch. "Not right for a man to carry that much weight, Cletus. I worry about you and that's a fact."

Carter nodded at him sternly and then went looking for Guild.

Cletus Baines stood in the dust looking resentful. How the hell could you enjoy a vanilla shake after a sermon like that?

Chapter Thirteen

Guild looked up at the big Ingram clock on the diner wall. In less than half an hour, Evans and Rittenauer would be leaving for the Adair ranch. He wasn't worried about them; he was worried about Sarah.

Guild was sipping his coffee and smoking a cigarette when he heard the counterman say, "Afternoon, Sheriff," then felt another person sit down on the adjoining stool.

"We need to talk," Sheriff Carter said.

Carter's tone surprised Guild. The Sheriff worked hard at seeming cool and in control. He looked sweaty now, and nervous. "Your woman."

"My woman?"

"The older one. You know."

"Sarah?"

"Right. Sarah."

"What about her?"

"Is she an emotional type?"

"Sometimes. But then, everybody is sometimes. Why?"

Instead of answering, Carter ordered coffee for himself. In the sunlight, you could see where alcohol had broken a few veins in his nose. The broken veins said that Carter probably wasn't as uncomplicated as he tried to seem.

"She just bought a gun at the general store."

"You sure it was Sarah?"

"Positive. Store clerk recognized her."

Guild spooned sugar into his coffee. "Wonder what the hell she wants a gun for?"

"That's what I'd like you to find out."

Guild looked over at him. "You sound worried."

"Is she good with a gun?"

"Not that I know of."

Now it was Carter's turn to stare hard at Guild. "You think she's capable of shooting somebody?"

"I suppose it would depend on who it is."

"One of them, most likely. Evans or Rittenauer."

Guild shrugged. A tightness had come into his chest. It was an unpleasant feeling. He was starting to worry more than he wanted to.

"How about you go talk to her, Guild?"

"Why not you?"

126

"One thing you learn about law enforcement, the first thing when a lawman shows up, people get riled. Sometimes it's better to send a friend. You're her friend."

"Yes, and right now maybe the only one she's got." He shook his head. He'd loved her for so many years that her grief became his. He could imagine her panic and anger now, seeing Frank Evans drawn to a gunfight he could never win.

"She's around here somewhere. How about finding her and talking to her."

Guild stood up. "You be at your office in half an hour?"

Carter nodded at the coffee. "I'll take care of your bill, Guild. You just go find her."

He went to her hotel and she wasn't there. He went to Frank Evans' hotel, but she wasn't there, either. Finally he tried Ben Rittenauer's hotel. The desk clerk said, "She was here about twenty minutes ago."

"Oh?"

"Looking for Mr. Rittenauer."

"He wasn't in?"

"No, he'd gone out about five minutes before she came."

"Any idea where he might have gone?"

The clerk shrugged. "Sorry but I don't."

He went up and down the board sidewalks, looking in the windows of restaurants and retail stores and ice cream parlors and general stores; he didn't see either one of them.

By now, he had decided why she would have bought a gun. No matter how Frank Evans treated her, she'd never shoot him. She was bound to him in some blood way that Guild could understand, because that's how he was bound to her. Even after she'd left him, he hadn't been able to hate her, at least not in the proper way shorn lovers usually hated the other person.

No, she would have bought a gun so she could kill Ben Rittenauer. Ben was the real threat to her life. For ten thousand dollars, and because Frank had helped make a fool of him, Ben was going to gun down Frank Evans and walk away — untouched by the law and a rich man.

Ben was the man she was going to kill.

Sarah saw Leo walk up to the barber shop and look in through the window. She sank back into the shadows of the alley. She'd been hiding there so she could have a good view of the barber shop's front door across the street.

She couldn't see how this could be a coincidence. Why would Leo just show up this way?

The barbershop smelled of wet hair and sweet hair tonic and talcum and cigar smoke. There was a wooden Indian just inside the door. He bore a tomahawk and a scowl and seemed to look with vast disapproval on what he saw in here.

Three men sat playing pinochle at a small table in the east corner. One of them was just now spitting tobacco into a filthy brass spittoon at his feet. The two players facing Guild looked up when he came in, but neither showed much interest in him.

Four other men, idlers, sat in the chairs rowed against the back wall. They had dumb hick grins on their faces and genuine mendacity in their eyes.

There were two barber chairs, both in use. In one a man was got up like a mummy, the barber sheet all the way up to his neck and a steaming towel wrapped over his face.

In the other chair, a short, bald man was shaving Ben Rittenauer's sideburns with a wicked-looking straight razor. Straight razors had always scared the hell out of Leo Guild.

Rittenauer saw him, of course. Was in

fact staring straight at him with great curiosity.

The barber was saying, "This'll be some payday for you, Mr. Rittenauer. Ten thousand dollars. You ever had a payday like this before?"

"Not as sweet as this one," Rittenauer said expansively. He was still eyeing Guild. "There's probably a damn good reason you're here. I just can't think of what it could be."

"We need to talk," Guild said.

"Seems we've had our talk."

"Something's come up."

"This here is a friend of Frank Evans'," Rittenauer said to the barber.

"You know better than that."

"Isn't that why you came here?" Rittenauer was enjoying himself, showing off for the rubes in the shop. "To find some way of calling off the fight so I won't kill poor Frank."

Rittenauer had his lady back and the prospect of ten thousand dollars in cash. Guild would probably be expansive, too.

"I'll just wait," Guild said.

Guild went over, sat down, and lit a cigarette. He blew smoke idly into the dust motes of the soft late afternoon sunlight coming through the window.

The rubes looked at each other and then at Guild and Rittenauer. Obviously they wished they knew what the hell was going on here. This was going to make some story in the taverns for many nights to come.

Guild smoked and watched the barber shave Ben Rittenauer. He was good, fast and scary, especially when he moved down to the throat. Rittenauer didn't look afraid in the least. When a barber got to that part on him, Guild always kept his fingers on the handle of his .44. Just in case.

"You want a shave?" the other barber asked him when his customer got up. The barber started brushing the man off with an almost comically long whisk broom.

"No thanks."

"Haircut, then?"

"No, thanks."

"You just going to sit here, then?"

"Looks that way, doesn't it?"

The barber muttered something under his breath, and then busied himself gussying up his station.

Sarah would reason with him and he'd finally see and agree with her reasoning. How it would be better for everybody if Beth and he would just get on the train and get out of town. No gunfight out at Adair's ranch, nothing like that at all. Just a nice quick train trip to a new location and a new life.

And after they had left by train, so would Sarah and Frank. There was a time when that had been their favorite treat, going on train trips. And it would be like that again. Only better. Because Frank was older and more mature, and this time there wouldn't be that sick-in-the-stomach, twitching-hands anxiety every time he saw a new pretty face. Because now Frank was beyond that. He would see, by the end of this day, how true her love was, how important her love was. Then he would be the Frank she'd always wanted, the safe Frank, the kind Frank, the loving Frank.

This would all come true as soon as Ben Rittenauer left the barber shop and she could talk to him a minute or two.

Rittenauer said, still in the barber chair, "I take it you heard about Beth."

"I heard."

"I knew she'd come back. She always does."

"I'm happy for you."

Rittenauer grinned. "You don't think much of her, do you?"

"Not when there are women like Sarah around."

"Isn't that the same Sarah who left you for Frank Evans?"

"That still doesn't make her like Beth."

Anger showed in Rittenauer's face. "I'd go real easy on Beth if I was you, friend."

"I'll remember that."

Guild knew not to push it anymore. He'd had his say. You didn't push a man like Ben Rittenauer about his woman. That was just crazy.

She'd be in a picture hat and Frank would be in a suit. They'd be walking along the bay in San Francisco, and there'd be vast white-sailed schooners in the gentle blue waters and summer green trees against the blue sky in the hills surrounding the bay.

And Sarah would know peace again — she would sleep nights through, and have her old appetite back. She would not lie in the darkness and sob so uselessly for hours — she would know peace again. And Frank — Frank would know peace for the first time in his life.

"Don't make me smell like a whore."

"No, sir, Mr. Rittenauer."

"A little bit of that stuff does just fine."

"Yes, sir, Mr. Rittenauer."

Guild had to agree with Rittenauer about that. Barbers always put so much bay rum on you, you smelled like a walking cathouse.

The barber was careful — some might say scared careful — with the bay rum and even more careful with the whisk broom.

Rittenauer walked over to the mirror and had a look at himself. "Handsome son of a bitch, aren't I?" he said to Guild's reflection.

"Downright beautiful."

Rittenauer turned back to the barber. "Here you go," he said. He gave the man a decent tip, too.

"Good luck, Mr. Rittenauer," the barber said.

Rittenauer put on his white hat. "You should be telling that to Frank Evans."

"Reckon I should be," the barber said.

Rittenauer nodded to the idlers. They looked as thrilled as young girls that a famous gunfighter would take any kind of note of them at all.

"You boys be good," Rittenauer said.

They all grinned their hateful hick grins and nodded their heads.

Outside on the walk, Rittenauer said,

"Why the hell are you getting involved in this, Guild?"

Guild said, "She bought a gun."

"Who bought a gun?"

"Sarah."

"Goddamn. You're kidding."

"Nope. And you know damn well who she'll try and use it on."

Sounding hurt, Rittenauer said, "Guild, what the hell did I ever do to her?"

"You're about to shoot the man she loves."

Rittenauer shook his head. "You ever considered the possibility that she's crazy?"

"I've considered it."

They were forty steps down the block from the barber's shop when a voice behind them called, "Mr. Rittenauer. Could you hold on a minute, please?"

Rittenauer said, just before he turned around, "Shit. It's her."

As Guild turned, seeing her now, he thought of what Rittenauer had just said about Sarah being crazy. She sure looked that way at the moment — drawn, fatigued, her gaze unfocused somehow, as if she were seeing ghosts and not people.

Guild's gaze dropped to her purse. She had her hand stuffed inside. He didn't have to wonder what she was holding in there.

"Afternoon, Sarah," Rittenauer said, somewhat grandly, given the situation.

"You smell wonderful," Sarah said. Her voice was flutey and girlish and sad.

"Sarah —" Guild started to say.

"I wondered if we could talk, Mr. Rittenauer."

Rittenauer glanced at Guild then back to Sarah. "I don't see why not, Sarah. As long as you quit calling me Mr. Rittenauer. Ben'll do fine."

Sarah went right on. "Ben, I want you to have a happy life."

"I appreciate that, Sarah."

"You and Beth will be able to start all over again."

"I certainly hope so."

"So, you shouldn't risk the gunfight this afternoon. You should leave town before it starts, forget all about it."

Rittenauer frowned in Guild's direction, then said to Sarah, "I appreciate your advice and your concern, Sarah."

She smiled. "I knew you'd see the right way, Ben."

Guild started circling, tiny steps that brought him closer to Sarah.

"But I'm afraid I can't do that, Sarah," Rittenauer was saying.

"But why not?"

"Because I need the money. I'm not any different from Frank. I'm just another broken-down gunfighter. I don't have a hundred dollars to my name."

Guild took a few more steps. Sarah was pulling again on the object inside her purse.

"Don't you love Beth?" Sarah said.

"Of course I do."

"Then why put her through this?"

"She wants the money, too."

"It's not fair," Sarah said.

"I'm sorry," Rittenauer said.

Just then Guild grabbed her.

He got her shooting arm good and tight and pulled her to him. "Give it to me, Sarah."

She tried to fight him. "No, Leo, you leave me alone."

"Come on, Sarah. You know how you hate people to stare."

And people were staring, crowding on the sidewalk now to see the gunny Rittenauer watch a man and woman fight each other.

She jerked away from Guild and got the Colt out before he could stop her.

The crowd was excited; almost grateful to the woman for providing such a show. They fanned out even wider now. Stray bullets killed as many people as carefully aimed ones.

In the sunlight, the barrel of the Colt looked long and all business. She held it with a steady hand. "I'm giving you a choice, Ben."

"Put it away, Sarah. I'm warning you." Ben's face had gone quickly from concern and kindness to hard anger. Nobody should ever pull a gun on Ben Rittenauer. When that happened, he was all reflex, a man with only one thought: kill the other person.

Rittenauer's hand dropped to the walnut handle of his gun.

"He isn't fooling, Sarah," Guild said.

"I want you to promise me that you won't fight Frank," Sarah said.

Obviously she had the impression that because she held a gun on Rittenauer, he could do nothing. But Guild knew that a man like Rittenauer could draw and fire in the time it would take Sarah to get one shot off.

"Sarah," Guild said softly. He stood at her side. He had only one chance to stop her. He got himself ready.

"She mustn't love you if she'd let you fight, Ben," Sarah said.

"I don't talk to anybody who's holding a

gun on me," Rittenauer said.

He glanced at Guild. He could see what Guild was about to do. He still kept his hand on the handle of his .44.

Guild moved. In two steps, he was knocking into her and slapping her wrist hard; the gun fell from her hand. It discharged, the bullet ripping into a piece of the overhanging roof to Sarah's right. The single shot was loud and ringing in Guild's ears, and the smell of gunsmoke was tart in his nostrils.

Ben Rittenauer came right up to her and pushed his face into hers. "That was a goddamn foolish thing to do, Sarah. Don't ever point a gun at a man like me, do you understand?" He was so angry, he was trembling.

But if Sarah heard or understood, she didn't let on. She stood dazed, staring at something distant that only she seemed able to see.

Rittenauer took his face from hers and said to Guild, "Get her out of here, Leo. She was lucky she didn't get killed."

Guild nodded and said gently to Sarah, "Come on. I'll buy you some coffee."

She was crying. "I don't want any coffee, Leo. I just want you to leave me alone. He's going to kill Frank this afternoon and you don't give one good damn."

She fell gently into Guild's chest, still crying. Above her head, Guild looked at Rittenauer. The man seemed to be losing his anger. He once more looked sorry for Sarah. He shook his head then walked off. Most of the onlookers watched him. Not even a crying woman was as big a draw as a gunfighter.

"You shouldn't've stopped me," Sarah said into Guild's chest.

"I'm glad I did."

"But he's going to kill Frank."

"That's their business, Sarah."

She started sobbing again. The crowd seemed to love sobbing almost as much as it did gunplay.

"But I love him so much," Sarah said into Guild's chest. "You can't know how much, Leo. You can't know."

Chapter Fourteen

Frank Evans was out behind the livery stable. The black man who worked there had set up bottles and cans on the top railing of the small corral for Evans to shoot off. At the sound of the first shot a small crowd of kids had gathered and now watched Evans put round after round into the targets.

"My pop says Ben Rittenauer'll kill him easy," one kid said.

Another kid said, "My old man's betting three dollars on Rittenauer. My ma said she's never seen him bet that much before."

Evans, who heard all this, kept shooting, of course. You couldn't let some goddamn kids get to you.

The dusty sunlight was richer now as late afternoon turned to dusk. An old roan, sad-eyed as only a dying horse can be, watched Evans from inside the corral; a sweet-natured collie sat a few feet from him. Every once in awhile, when the chatter of the children and the bright, vivid loss of Beth got to him again, Evans would lean down and pet the collie. Back on the farm, he'd had an animal this sweet and loyal and true, and every time he petted this animal he thought of Sarah, because she was also sweet and loyal and true.

Then he'd think maybe he should get on the train, the way Rittenauer suggested, and hold Sarah's hand till they were in some new land all shiny with promise and hope. He did not want to die, in fact was quite afraid to die. The irony was that, with Beth gone, he felt dead already. He wanted to cry, right here in front of the goddamn kids, bawl his eyes out because he felt sick inside, sick in a way no disease could ever make him feel, the sickness of irreparable loss.

"See, I tole ya. He ain't fer shit. He missed that can clean. Sh—it. Fancy fuckin' gunny."

The kid, a towhead with freckles and big buck teeth, spoke these words at exactly the wrong time. Because Evans could no longer abide them crowding him this way with the stupid opinions they'd gotten from their parents.

He whirled, thrusting his gun back into his holster, and picked up the loudmouth by the front of his shirt, slamming him against the oak tree that provided leafy shade for the horses.

"You say that to my face, you punk, and see what happens!"

But before the chubby twelve-year-old could say anything — he was just dangling there in Evans' iron grip — an ironic male voice said, "My, my, Mr. Evans. One would surely hope that your nerves are steadier when you face Mr. Rittenauer this evening."

Evans turned to see Tom Adair's man Hollister walking toward him. There was a certain switch in his gait and a certain sweetness in his smile that troubled Evans. Maybe being around a powerful, angry man all the time made you into a woman.

Evans set the boy down.

The boy said, "He's gonna kill you, Evans. Just like my old man says."

"Then you can come out to the cemetery and piss on my grave, can't you?" Evans said harshly.

All the other boys laughed. Evans asked, "Anybody here think I'm going to beat Rittenauer?"

No hands showed.

Evans looked at Hollister. "Somebody could make a lot of money betting on me."

"Yeah," the chubby towhead said, "but you ain't gonna win."

"You boys git now," the old black man said. Even in this heat he wore his coarse blue button-up sweater. He was the color of mahogany, and he had eyes as brown and sad as the roan in the corral. "Git and git good and git now," he said again, clapping his hands as if he were scattering chickens.

The boys ran away, tossing curse words over their shoulders.

Hollister said, "I thought I'd come over and offer you a ride out to the ranch."

"I can find my own ride." There was a harshness in Evans' voice. Definitely something about Hollister that he didn't like or trust. "Anyway, that isn't why you're here."

"It isn't?"

"No. You wanted to see if I was gonna go through with it."

The too-sweet smile was back on Hollister's too-sweet lips. "You're a very observant man, Mr. Evans."

"Well, for your information, I'm not backing out. I'm going out to Adair's ranch and get that ten thousand dollars."

Hollister said, the smile almost but not quite gone, "I'm told the woman went back to him. What's her name — Beth?"

Evans could have gotten angry, even slapped Hollister for pushing him this way. But he just said, "You like to push people, don't you, Mr. Hollister?"

Hollister smiled. "I suppose I do, now that you mention it."

"Be careful who you push," Evans said. "They might push back."

He left Hollister standing there. He went back to his room to wash up for the ride out to the Adair ranch.

By 1886 it had all started to end for many large cattle ranchers. With bank failures and big Eastern investors nervous about the cattle industry, dollars were tight and banker lending boards conservative. And without a banker, and a ready line of credit, even the most swaggering of cattlemen were reduced to meekness.

Tom Adair remained the exception. His ranch claimed nearly 800,000 acres in four different counties, with nearly 95,000 head of cattle. It was boasted — at least by Adair himself in moments of whiskey pride — that he had invested in more than 4,000 miles of barbed wire to keep his claim inviolate. When he stood on the hill where he'd buried two generations of blood kin, including an irascible yet beloved father, everything he saw sprawling to the line of the horizon belonged to him.

The ranch house itself was the centerpiece of his spread, a Victorian fortress so exotic in its layout and decoration that a woman from Chicago had taken a train out here just so she could write about it for her newspaper. Adair liked to stand on the hill just at dawn and look at the sun rising just over the edge of the spired roof. In the early morning, the red roof tiles were still damp with dew and they shone like fire in the slanting golden sun rays.

Because of the ranch, he'd become a favorite of the wealthy and the powerful. A short-haul train line had built a leg of track that came within six miles of the westernmost edge of his spread. Surreys, stagecoaches, and wagons picked up an unending stream of passengers, important men in dark suits, walrus mustaches, and top hats; women beautiful in bustles and picture hats and small steady smiles meant to please.

Many nights, beneath an arc of midnight sky and furious western stars, violin music could be heard on the prairies. Or there was the voice of a celebrated diva, or the lively cadences of a marching band, the trumpets bright as Fourth of July fireworks.

You could tell a rancher's importance by the kind of people he could attract to his ranch. Tom Adair, twice married, twice divorced, restless, a man who'd once paid a Negro one hundred dollars to shoot three Chinese in cold blood because one of Adair's friends had never actually seen a living person die — Adair got only the top of the list, from governors to businessmen to the whores most popular in any given season.

Yet for all the amusements he'd brought to his ranch, the gunfight this evening was perhaps his best idea yet. As the guests arrived throughout the day, he teased each with a promise of "something very special tonight." His guests knew enough to be excited. If Tom Adair said something was very special, it would indeed be.

Down by the horse barns there was a big corral where Adair often staged rodeos, particularly in the fall when breeding stock was being rotated. It was here that he had built a small grandstand, replete with colorful pennant crackling in the cool prairie winds. The grandstand, as he never tired of pointing out, easily sat two hundred.

Tonight, inside the corral and directly in front of the grandstand, Adair would have

Rittenauer and Evans face off.

He stood in the center of the corral now. The Mexes had combed the dirt this morning, raking it free of horseshit and pieces of broken horseshoes.

He stood in the dusty sunlight imagining how it would happen tonight: the two men at opposite ends of the vast corral, the tense crowd watching rapturously, the men drawing closer, closer, and then the sound of gunfire, one man beginning to crumble a few moments after the shots were fired.

Would they ever stop talking about it? He could hear them now in their dens and country clubs and salons. Did anybody ever give better parties than handsome Tom Adair? Why, did you hear about the night he had a gunfight staged right on his own ranch? And a man actually died?

Now, as he circled the corral, looking up at the grandstand from the point of view of the gunmen, he thought of his father and how much the old man had hated rich people. Even when the old man had owned as many as twenty banks, he still thought of himself as poor and oppressed. And he'd lived that way, too, washing his clothes again and again till they were rags, whining when the day came to buy new ones, and never buying anything fancy for the house when a perfectly functional version of the thing could be had from Sears, Roebuck or Montgomery Wards.

The old man certainly wouldn't have enjoyed himself here tonight. Not his sort of folks.

But for Tom Adair, tonight would be a golden moment. Never before at one party had he had two senators and a governor.

If people didn't know that Tom Adair was important before, they would certainly know it tonight.

He took one more look up at the grandstand.

My God, he could hear their screams and shouts now. When the gunfight started. When one of the men fell down dead.

Oh, no, they'd never quit talking about what they saw this evening. In every fashionable gathering place from Ohio to California, Tom Adair's ingenuity as a host would be celebrated.

Even above the prairie winds now, he heard it; the gunfire as it would be tonight.

Then he went to greet a newly arrived stage, just in time to glimpse the nicely turned leg of a woman stepping down to join the other guests already off the stage.

"You must be Tom," she said, in a discreetly flirtatious way, obviously impressed equally with his good looks and the ranch.

"Yes, yes, I am," he smiled.

And he sounded quite happy, even smug about it, as if there could be no fate better than being Tom Adair.

"When's the last time you ate?"

"I'm not sure."

"Well, eat something now."

"I'm not hungry now."

"Eat anyway."

"Shut up, Leo. I'm sick of you talking."

There was nothing to say to that.

He sat silent and smoked his cigarette.

"You should have let me shoot him."

"No, I shouldn't," he said.

"He's going to kill Frank."

"Maybe."

"Maybe? You know he is, Leo."

Guild sighed. They were in a restaurant. In the late afternoon the place was hot and smelled of cooking grease. A man sat at the counter eating pork chops. His mouth and hands were greasy and he smacked his lips loudly as he ate, which irritated Guild irrationally. Guild wanted to go over and tell the guy to eat like a civilized man or throw down the chops and get the hell out of here.

From the pocket of his shirt, Guild took

a small blue ticket. He laid it in the center of their table.

Sarah looked at it. "What's this?"

"Ticket. Train ticket."

"That's what I figured."

"Train leaves in half an hour."

"To where?"

"East."

"Who do I know in the east?"

"You've got a sister in Maine."

"I haven't seen her in fifteen years."

"Maybe now's the time to go see her."

"You think I could just leave here knowing what's going to happen tonight?"

He smoked his cigarette some more.

"He's a better man than you think, Leo," she said.

He said nothing.

"You want to see him die, don't you, Leo?"

"You know better than that."

"Because of what he did to you. Or what you think he did. But it wasn't him, Leo. It was me. I was the one who hurt you."

The waitress and the man with the pork chops were pretending not to hear any of this. Right now, Guild didn't give a damn what they heard.

"Can we go see him, Leo?"

"For what?"

"To try and stop him."

"It won't do any good, Sarah."

"Just one more chance. Then I'll take your train ticket and I'll leave."

"You promise?"

"I promise."

He looked at her. "You really think he's worth it, Sarah?"

Very quietly, she said, "Yes, Leo, I think he is."

Guild sighed. "We don't even know where he is. Maybe he's already left for the ranch."

"I'll find him. He can't hide from me." She sounded young and excited now that she was going to see Frank again. And she sounded desperate.

"Train leaves in twenty minutes."

"I'll be on it. Just like I promised. And Frank'll be with me."

Now she sounded crazy. Guild felt sad for her, and somehow embarrassed, too, that she could believe such a thing. "He's going to come back to me, Leo. I know he is," she said.

Guild got up and went over to pay the bill. The waitress looked at him kind of funny but didn't say anything. She took his money and made change. She was slow, irritatingly so.

When Guild turned around again, the table where they'd been was empty. Sarah was gone.

Chapter Fifteen

Beth finished packing, two neat carpetbags to hold most of her things, and then went over to the table to write Frank a goodbye letter, that somebody would read to him. She had only gone through the third grade, but because she'd shown remarkable skill at penmanship and vocabulary, people generally took her to be much more educated than she was. Plus, there had been her mother's friend Eugene, a wealthy and respectable businessman who'd kept Beth and her mother for nearly six years, before his wife took sick and sheer guilt caused him to end the relationship.

Eugene had loved to share the fine education he'd had, teaching the "girls," as he always called them (as if they were sisters and not mother and daughter), a "smidge" about poetry, a smidge about literature, a smidge about classical music, and much more than a smidge about table manners and how one behaved in polite society.

Beth had been eight years old the first

time he took her in the bedroom and educated her in a very different area — showing her the things that pleased him in a physical way. This had confused her, of course. She'd been raised, marginally anyway, a Methodist and certainly Methodists wouldn't approve of such things, but when she went to her mother about it, all her mother said was, "Hon, don't you think it's the least we can do for somebody who treats us as well as Eugene does? Why, if it wasn't for Eugene, we wouldn't have this apartment or any of our dresses." Sometimes Eugene had liked it when they both pleased him at the same time. This had always seemed particularly shameful to Beth, but it didn't seem to bother her mother much at all.

After Eugene, they moved to St. Louis, where they met other men like Eugene, men of means and education, men strict and demanding about the way they liked to be pleased. By this time, Beth was a teenager and a beauty. Men got awfully silly about her. One young man, quite ugly and quite rich, hanged himself, it was said, because of her. Her mother always said that Beth was "the prize," the trophy that men wanted for themselves. To possess Beth was to mark a man as special.

When she was seventeen, her mother died of influenza. She still thought of how her mother looked laid out in the funeral home. Gone was all the beauty; gone was all the grace. The body was hard and cold and quite ugly. And she still remembered that nobody but the plump, effeminate funeral director was there. None of the respectable male friends who had kept them over the years so much as expressed sympathy. She had to find her own men now. At first it wasn't difficult, but somewhere between her nineteenth and twenty-fifth birthdays, she noticed that her beauty had begun to lose its sheen and luster. Oh, the bones were perfect still, and the grave lovely eyes burned as always with sad inscrutable promise, but the flesh itself . . .

This was not something she simply imagined, either. The men themselves became lesser, too, not quite so rich, not quite so educated, cruder in passion and pleasure. A few were even violent, something her mother would never have stood for. She saw what lay ahead for her, of course: the streets. Then she would be nothing more than one of the prostitutes she and her mother used to giggle about so uncharitably.

She left St. Louis and drifted west, lesser

men becoming lesser still. Then she'd met Ben Rittenauer, and for a time, things had been good.

She liked being associated with a gunfighter; even though he was beginning to bald, and a small protuberant pot was beginning to show above his belt line, there was something dignified about Ben that she liked very much. She felt protected by him. And he understood enough about women to let her cry when the terrible crying came; and he left her alone about sex, too. She didn't like sex, sex sometimes brought on the terrible crying in fact. And so she'd please him quickly and then lie there with him in the darkness and he wouldn't berate her at all for not enjoying herself.

Frank Evans had been the opposite. It seemed that sex was all he thought of. And so she'd pretended, as she had with all the rich men, that she enjoyed herself endlessly in bed. She saw now that Frank represented the last of her youth — he'd been dashing and loud and funny, and touchingly vulnerable in an odd, swaggering way. And tonight Ben would kill him.

In some ways, Frank might be better off. He was at the end of his road. He was losing his skills as a gunfighter, he was losing his looks, and he was losing his ability to make a purposeful life for himself. But still she felt guilty. He saw her going back to Ben as a betrayal. But it wasn't, not really. She was simply tired, and with Frank there was no rest. Tonight Ben would have ten thousand dollars, and they would take that money and set up the rest of their lives with it. They would be companions in old age. Frank would never understand that.

She wrote: *Goodbye, Frank. I wish we hadn't had that argument today. I'm not mad about you hitting me. I know how angry and hurt you are. I don't blame you. I'd be angry and hurt, too. But things have changed so much and I'm so tired; and I'm getting afraid, too, the way I was just after my mother died. I know you can't understand this. I know you don't believe that somewhere in my heart I still care about you, Frank. But it's true, it really is.*

She signed her name to it and left it on the bureau where he'd be sure to see it. Then she went over and picked up her carpetbags and left the hotel room for the last time.

Ben was waiting for her in the restaurant downstairs.

Sarah knocked twice on the hotel room door. There was no answer. But the desk clerk had told her he was still up here.

"Frank?"

No response.

"Frank?"

Still nothing.

A couple walked by laughing. Sarah wanted to slap the happiness from their faces. Their happiness seemed vulgar to her.

She tried one more time. "Frank?"

She tried the doorknob. Unlocked. She turned it sixty degrees and went inside.

He was on the bed, all his clothes on. His back was to her. A letter lay on the foot of the bed. The room was in shadow and smelled of dust.

"Are you all right, Frank?"

Then she saw the whiskey bottle on the stand next to the bed.

She felt great excitement. If he was drinking, that meant he was not going to go through with the fight after all. Frank never drank before a gunfight. Ever.

She went over and sat down on the bed. She put her hand on his back and began to rub the long muscles over his shoulder blades. The familiar smells of his hair and his body came to her, and she felt almost as if she would capsize. She'd been so long without him, and now here they were on a bed together.

"Frank," she said, and leaned forward to kiss him.

He turned over and looked at her finally. "Good old Sarah," he said. "Why the hell don't you just leave me alone?"

He'd had enough drink now to make him mean.

"I just wanted to make sure you were all right," she said.

"Good old Sarah," he repeated, putting as much emphasis on her name as he could.

"I'm glad you're not going to fight him."

He sat up and said, "What the hell are you talking about?"

She nodded toward the whiskey. "The bottle. You never drink before a fight."

He threw his legs off the bed, stood up, and grabbed the bottle. "Well, this one time I am. If it's any of your business, I mean."

"But Frank —"

"What the hell are you doing here, Sarah?"

"I just wanted to convince you to —" But she was hurt and flustered now and couldn't talk.

He came around the bed and took her arm so hard in his fingers that pain shot all the way down her side.

He dragged her to the door and said, "Get the hell out of here, Sarah. Right now."

"But, Frank —"

"You heard me, Sarah, out."

"But, Frank, I've given you most of my life. It's not fair. It's —"

The knock came. Frank pushed her out of the way and opened the door. Guild stood there.

"I came to get Sarah."

"Fine. I'm glad. I don't want her bothering me anymore."

Guild looked at Sarah. He said softly, "C'mon, Sarah. Let's go."

"Frank —" she started to say. But then stopped.

Guild said again, "C'mon, Sarah. Let's go."

The train smelled of heat and oil and steam. Porters were loading baggage, and passengers were saying their goodbyes.

Guild stood by the third car with Sarah. "Say hello to Ellen for me."

Sarah smiled wearily. "You two always got along, didn't you?"

"She's a fine woman."

"Thanks for coming up to Frank's room and getting me."

"Sure."

"I guess he really doesn't love me anymore, does he?"

She was trying hard to be brave about it.

"The summers are good in Maine. The ocean especially," Guild said.

"That will be nice, won't it?" she said. "The ocean, I mean?"

She looked old and frail and worn to the nub. Whatever dignity there was in her, and sometimes there was considerable dignity, seemed to have been replaced by sadness now.

Sarah glanced around the platform. "I guess I'll board."

"It won't be pulling out for another ten minutes. I'll be glad to wait."

"No," she said, leaning down and taking her bag. "I'll just go get a seat now. Maybe that way I can sit next to the window. You know how much I like to watch the scenery."

She started crying then, and he wasn't sure why. Probably lots of reasons really. He took her to him and held her with a great abiding reverence for all the things they'd meant to each other in their long confusing lives, from the days when he'd teased her as an eight-year-old, to the snowy nights when they'd snuggled for warmth in their marriage bed, to this day and this place and the strange and troubled woman she'd become since leaving him for Frank, the strange and troubled woman he nonetheless still loved.

"If I knew where you'd be, I'd write you a letter," she said, trying to stop her tears now.

"How about if I write you?"

"Ooh, that would be wonderful, Leo. Really."

He smiled. "Then I'll do it, Sarah. I promise."

Then she was on the train, at first lost in the white waving steam, and then reappearing, a small sweet face tucked into the corner of a window, a small hand waving goodbye.

Guild, numb, left the depot and went to get himself a drink.

Chapter Sixteen

Sarah watched Guild until he disappeared from the depot. Again, she was struck by how old he seemed these days; weary, really. He seemed to shamble instead of walk.

She sat there a long moment, letting the noises of the Pullman car fill her — the two bratty children racing up and down the aisle up front; the general din of conversation, mostly female; the clanking of another car being coupled on to the back; and an old man sitting behind her snoring wetly. Apparently he was deaf; none of the noise seemed to bother him.

The portly conductor came down the aisle asking for tickets. He had a small silver paper punch that he used with a great deal of self-satisfaction.

She handed him the ticket. Obviously taken with her prettiness, he said, "You have a nice trip for yourself, ma'am."

She mustered her best social smile. "I will. And thank you."

He touched the brim of his black kepi-style cap and strutted on down the aisle to the next seat.

She lay back and closed her eyes.

She tried to imagine Maine. She'd only been there once — in her early twenties, she'd been — and she thought of it now as miles of raw, beautiful coastline and dark, brambly woods. It would be good to see her sister Ellen, the resident optimist of the family. If anybody could help put Sarah's life back together, it would be Ellen.

The train jerked forward, preparatory to leaving the depot.

Up front, the two brats cried out joyously. They were at the age when all trips were grand adventures.

She wished she could be like them, the children. Live only in the present. Think only of Maine and Ellen. There might even be a new man there to meet.

The conductor was leaning out of the car, shouting "Board!" to the last stragglers as they hurried across the platform burdened down with luggage.

All at once, Sarah bolted. She jumped up from her seat, grabbed her luggage, and moved out into the aisle. She'd taken no more than four steps when she ran into the conductor's considerable bulk.

"Ma'am, the train's about to leave."

"I know."

"Shouldn't you sit down?"

"I've decided — not to go."

"Oh?" She could see in his eyes that he was now classifying her as something other than a pretty older woman. She had become a low-grade nuisance.

"He's gathering steam," the conductor said. "I can't have him stop now."

"I know."

Beneath her, the train rumbled forward again.

"Please let me by," she said. "Please."

Shaking his head, looking for sympathy from the onlookers who were now also regarding her as a nuisance, he pulled himself back so she could squeeze past his bulk.

"Thank you," she said, and hurried forward, banging her luggage against his knee as she passed him.

By the time she reached the Pullman's door, the train was actually moving — she felt the boxy car start to sway side to side. Out the window, the depot was beginning to retreat.

She moved down to the bottom step and jumped, landing comically on the depot platform. Sprawled over her luggage, she pushed herself awkwardly to her feet. Two men rushed to help her up.

"You took a real chance there, ma'am," one of the men said, obviously wanting to scold her, as if she were a disobedient child. "That was a foolish thing to do."

"I know," she said, as she gained her feet again. "But then I'm a foolish sort of person."

She picked up her luggage and walked into the depot.

The clerk at the general store was waiting on an old man looking for an elixir for his rheumatism. No matter what bottle the clerk showed him, the old man shook his head, his snowy white hair flying out from his long, narrow skull. "T'ain't it, Cletus, t'ain't it at all."

So Cletus would climb up the stepladder and tug down another dusty bottle of another potent elixir and show it to the old man. The old man would promptly shake his head again.

She wondered where Cletus found all his patience.

Finally, seeming to run out of patience, Cletus said, "Henry."

"Yes?"

"You know how many bottles I've showed you?"

"How many?"

"Sixteen."

"I'll be dagged."

"Henry?"

"What?"

"I ain't going to show you no more."

"You ain't?"

"Nope. Now you go find your wife and bring her back."

"How come?"

" 'Cause she'll know what you're looking for."

"She will?"

Cletus sighed. "She's across the street at Lyman's, looking at hats. Now you go get her."

"All right, Cletus. If you say so."

Cletus walked around the counter, took Henry by the elbow, and walked him toward the front door. From there he pointed across the street.

"Over at Lyman's," he said again. He half shouted.

"Much obliged, Cletus."

And with that, the old man doddered out.

"It's a darn shame," Cletus said, coming back around the counter. "Henry ain't been the same since he turned 95." He seemed to look at her for the first time, recognizing her. "Oh," he said.

"You told the sheriff about the gun I bought."

"Had to, ma'am. Sheriff Carter wants me to tell him about every gun I sell. And right away, too, or he gets darn mad."

"I need another gun."

"Ma'am?"

"I need another one."

He hesitated and then said, "There was almost some trouble. With Ben Rittenauer, I mean."

She said nothing, just stared at him.

"I can't do it, ma'am."

She put twenty-five dollars down on the counter.

"Oh, ma'am."

"You're tempted, aren't you?"

"Ma'am, I'm just a clerk here. I don't own this store and I sure don't see that kind of money. Not very often, anyway."

She put more money on the counter.

"Oh, ma'am," he said.

"You have kids?"

"Three of them."

"Bet you don't often get to buy them gifts."

"Not often. But please don't tempt me this way."

"You have debts?"

"Everybody has debts, ma'am."

"Bet it would be nice to pay on a couple of them with money like this."

"Oh, ma'am, please don't —"

She put down a few more dollars.

"There's no reason anybody ever has to know," she said.

He swallowed hard. "What're you plannin' to do with the gun?"

"I'm not sure yet."

He looked down at the money.

"Wouldn't your wife be surprised?" Sarah said.

He looked up at her, looking as if he were about to cry.

"And wouldn't she be grateful, seeing you bring in extra money like this?"

He put out a tentative hand, like a child putting his fingers dangerously close to a fire, and said, "She sure would be grateful, ma'am. She sure would."

Hollister picked them up in front of Ben Rittenauer's hotel in a wagon, with three broad seats behind him, beneath a surrey roof.

Beth and Ben appeared first. The small crowd that had gathered in front of the hotel remarked on how pretty she looked. Ben looked nothing special — neither

170

swaggering nor afraid. He helped his lady up into the wagon and then sat down himself, both behind Hollister. They didn't say anything, just sat there staring straight ahead.

Frank Evans was five minutes late. He wore a clean white shirt and custom-tailored trousers. His holster, extra-long and fancy, was tied down with a showy piece of rawhide. He walked over to the wagon and climbed up beside Hollister. Somebody in the crowd shouted, "Only one of you boys're comin' back. You realize that?"

Nobody in the wagon seemed to hear.

The wagon pulled out. The horse in the traces had left enough dung to keep the hungry flies busy till dawn.

Guild tried to play pinochle. He went three hands before he realized it was hopeless. Cards required concentration, especially pinochle, and he couldn't concentrate. He kept thinking about Sarah on the train and Rittenauer and Evans out at the Adair ranch. Poor men shouldn't die for the amusement of rich men.

He excused himself from the card table and went back to the bar. Two men his age were telling Civil War stories. They were Union men and without apologies for it.

The stories started out reasonable enough but soon became whoppers. Guild hated whoppers. There wasn't any tension in them; in whoppers, anything could happen and usually did.

After two sudsy beers, he had a whiskey. Guild rarely had whiskey.

At the livery stable, she bought a bay. The black man who sold it to her brought her out back, helped her up on the animal, and then instructed her on the fastest way to reach the Adair spread from there.

She left town just as the air began to turn muzzy with dusk. The hooves of her mount were loud in the supper time silence.

Chapter Seventeen

Promptly at six, Cletus closed the store, pulling down the front blinds, double-checking the safe, and setting up the new red licorice display for the kids tomorrow. He took his usual route out the backdoor to the alley.

If you walked five sandy blocks straight down the alley, you'd reach the backyard of Cletus' house.

Tonight, walking, he whistled.

Usually at day's end he was so fatigued, he thought of nothing except supper and sitting in the parlor in his stocking feet and having his youngest girl rub his toes. How she loved to do that, sweet child that she was.

But tonight Cletus looked and sounded ten years younger. It was the money in his pocket, of course. His wife was really going to be surprised. He'd already made up his mind that he wasn't going to tell her where it came from. He'd lie and say that Mr. Sanford, the owner of the store, had given him the money as a bonus, unlikely a tale as it was.

So he whistled. When he saw a sweet collie, he stopped to pet her. And when he saw a woman taking down white bedsheets from her clothesline, he waved.

He was half a block away from home when he stopped whistling.

A single, simple thought had just hit him: I'm not a lucky man. I've been blessed with a true-blue wife and three wonderful children, but I have not been blessed with luck. I'm not strong; I'm not handsome; I'm not successful. And I will get caught. Somehow, Sheriff Carter will find out what I've done and he'll come after me. Then, Lord, I'll be looking for a new job, one where I have no responsibility with firearms, and my wife will be frying shit sandwiches because that'll be the only thing to eat.

He turned sharply around in the sandy alley and went back to the downtown area. The red sun was sinking just on the sharp black edge of a garage roof.

"Sheriff."

"Howdy, Cletus."

"Sheriff, you have a minute?"

"I was just going over to the café for some supper. Care to walk along?"

Bolder than he'd ever been, Cletus closed the door behind him, shutting the two men inside the sheriff's office.

The sheriff looked amused with Cletus' new boldness. "This must be important."

"It is."

"Then go ahead."

"Sheriff, I've made a mistake."

"All right."

"A bad one."

"I see."

"I accepted a bribe."

Sheriff Carter smiled. "No offense, Cletus, but who the hell'd want to bribe you?"

"That woman."

"What woman?"

"The one who almost shot Ben Rittenauer this afternoon."

"Just what the hell are you trying to tell me, anyway?" For the first time, the sheriff looked interested in all this. Now, instead of sitting back, he was hunched forward, elbows on his desk.

"I sold her another gun."

"What?"

"Yes. And I'm sorry."

"Why in God's name would you do something like that?"

"Because I was greedy."

"Son of a bitch."

"I knew you'd get mad and I'm sorry."

"When did this happen?"

"About forty-five minutes ago."

"Son of a bitch."

"Like I said, I'm sorry."

The sheriff stood up. "You may just have gotten a man killed tonight, Cletus."

"I realize that."

"That was a dumb goddamn thing to do."

"That's why I came over here. To tell you."

Sheriff Carter put on his fancy hat and started for the door. "You say she bribed you?"

"Yessir."

"How much?"

Cletus told him.

"What're you going to do with it?" the sheriff asked.

Cletus took the bills from his pocket and offered them to the sheriff. "Hand it over."

The lawman looked at the money in Cletus' hand. "I imagine your wife and kids could use that, couldn't they?"

"Yessir."

"Then you keep it and take it home."

"But —"

"Somebody might as well get something

good out of this whole goddamned mess."

And with that, Carter pushed his way out of the office and into the dusky street.

His hand wouldn't quit twitching. He kept making it into a fist so Hollister wouldn't see.

"You all right, Mr. Evans?" Hollister asked, working the traces as the horses moved swiftly toward the Adair ranch. There was amusement in his voice. He could see how anxious Evans was and he was enjoying it.

"How about you, Mr. Rittenauer?"

"Me?"

"Yes."

"I'm doing fine."

And he sounded fine, too. He really did.

Hollister looked over at Evans and smiled. "Did you hear that, Mr. Evans? Rittenauer is doing fine."

Evans didn't reply, just stared straight ahead. He should have gotten his own ride out to the ranch. Being this close to Beth wasn't good. He wanted to turn around and shout at her about how she'd betrayed him.

His hand started twitching again, his gun hand.

Hollister said, "It won't be long now,

Mr. Evans. It won't be long now at all."

He hitched the horses faster.

The bar was filling up for the evening when the sheriff came in. Everybody was talking about the fight out at the ranch. Almost nobody felt that Evans could win. Everybody was talking about how Ben Rittenauer had once killed one of the Bremer brothers. Anybody who could kill one of the Bremer brothers didn't have anything to worry about from Frank Evans.

Guild was at the bar when the sheriff came up. He had to elbow his way up to Guild. The men were drunk enough now that they were no longer intimidated by a lawman's badge.

"You're going to need that drink, Guild," the sheriff said, pouring himself a shot from Guild's bottle of rye.

"Oh. How's that?"

Before he spoke, the sheriff downed his whiskey with great efficiency and poured himself a second. He didn't ask permission this time either.

The sheriff said, "You put her on the train."

"That's right."

"But she didn't stay on the train."

"What?!"

The sheriff shook his head. "She got off the train and went straight back to the general store and bribed the clerk into selling her another gun."

"I'll be goddamned."

"Then she went over to the livery stable and got herself a horse."

This time it was Guild who shook his head. "How long ago?"

"Half-hour, from what I can figure."

"You riding out there?"

The sheriff nodded. "Thought you might want to go along."

Without asking, the lawman poured each of them one more drink.

They raised their glasses and threw them back.

"She's a damned determined woman," the sheriff said.

"She always was," Guild said.

They left.

When she reached the ranch, Sarah found more than two hundred people dressed in fancy dresses and evening clothes spread out across the rolling, shorn grass on the west side of the huge house. She'd reached the ranch before the wagon because the liveryman had told her of a shortcut that only a horse could handle.

In the dusk, the first stars were coming out, the glass lanterns were beautiful against the sky, and the air was fresh with the scent of mown grass.

The guests were loud with laughter and their own self-importance. She had no trouble slipping among them to reach the house.

Once inside, she went straight back to the kitchen. She wished there were time to stop and look at all the lovely furnishings and the paintings on the walls, or to watch the string quartet in the library tuning their instruments and trading soft, smart jokes.

In the kitchen a small group of white, Mexican, and Indian women were busily preparing dinner. Outside the screen door a huge side of beef turned over and over on a fiery spit. Without a word, she grabbed a white apron and started helping. She was pleased with her own ingenuity. Nobody would question why she moved among the crowd.

The gun was in a deep pocket in the folds of her dress. When the time came, when she could get a clear shot at Ben Rittenauer, she would be ready.

Beth wished the wagon ride would never end. She wanted to go right on past the ranch to someplace golden and magical, someplace that her mother would have liked and admired, where older men with white walrus mustaches took care of young girls like Beth.

But despite the vividness of her daydreams, Beth kept looking at Frank Evans' back, at how he was half slumped-over and his right hand kept trembling. He knew he was going to die in an hour or so, and Beth felt more pity for him than she wanted to. He had been an abusive lover and a cold friend, and yet she saw his desperation and insecurity, had always recognized it as much like her own desperation and insecurity. She wanted to put her hand on his and say gently, I'm still your friend, Frank. I'm better off with Ben. But I'm still your friend.

The wagon clattered on into the chilling night.

Back in her daydream she imagined someplace wonderful, imagined herself floating into a ballroom in a dress that would shame a princess. And the men would watch her so admiringly.

With perfect mean satisfaction Hollister said, "That hand of yours is starting to shake pretty bad, Mr. Evans. You want a drink from my flask?"

Before she even knew what she was saying, Beth heard her own voice. "Leave him alone, Hollister. You've been picking on him all the way out here."

Ben was looking at her — curious, maybe even angry.

"Just sit back and relax, Beth. He's no concern of yours anymore," he said gently.

Hollister turned around and looked at her, the same cold smile as always on his face. Hollister was having himself one fine time.

He sped up the horses and the wagon rushed on into the darkening night.

Chapter Eighteen

Sarah was carrying a tray of glasses from the kitchen to a picnic table out under a chestnut tree when she saw, far down the dusty access road leading to the house, the black surrey. She paused, squinting her eyes so that she could see who was in the wagon. She recognized Frank sitting next to the driver. Frank. She felt sick and exhilarated at the same time. She wanted to run to him and tell him to go back, go back, tell him they could start all over again, that there was still time to get out.

"Hey!" the bosswoman said. "Hurry up! There's no time to lollygag!"

Sarah rushed the glasses over to the table, nearly stumbling in the process. That would be a nice pickle; to stumble and shatter all those glasses; then she'd be exposed for who she really was.

"Look, everybody!" a voice shouted to the red and yellow and gray streaks of dusk sky. "Look! It's Hollister and he's bringing back the gunfighters!"

All Sarah could think of was the way the crowd had reacted the time Sarah Bernhardt — her favorite actress — had arrived at the train station in Denver. How they'd pushed to see the actress. There'd been something almost frightening about it. The way there was now. Nearly two hundred people formed a circle around the surrey when it pulled up near the ranch house.

Despite several hours of liquor, the guests were curiously subdued. They were just looking, staring.

Tom Adair, in a fancy red brocade evening jacket, eased his way to the front of the crowd, grabbed hold of the surrey, and helped himself up onto the first step.

"Ladies and gentlemen, these are the folks we've been waiting for!"

The crowd burst into applause and excited shouts. At the moment, Tom Adair sounded and looked like a circus barker.

"I'd like to ask the two men to stand up when I introduce them," Adair cried. "And be sure to give each of them a nice greeting."

Adair stepped down so that the people in the surrey could get out of the wagon.

As Frank Evans stood up, Adair said, "This is Frank Evans, whom we've all heard so much about!"

This was the only time in Sarah's memory that the adulation of a crowd made Frank Evans look uncomfortable. On the second step down, he froze and ducked his head, his eyes averting from the noise and the crowd.

"And now here comes Ben Rittenauer and his lady friend!" Adair sang out, once more sounding like a shill introducing a carnival act.

As Frank pushed his way through the crowd, Beth and Ben came down the steps. Rittenauer handled the moment a lot better than Frank had. He stood on the ground shaking a few hands and letting drunks pat him on the back and shout out good luck.

Sarah turned, looking for Frank.

She saw him over by one of the tables, where a Negro in a white jacket was pouring whiskey for men and punch for women.

Frank took a shot and quickly knocked it back.

Adair led Beth and Ben over to the same table. Beth took a little punch. Ben declined anything.

Adair then stood with the three people as if they were all posing for a picture. As the four of them faced the crowd, Adair said, "You'd better get over to the main corral if you want seats." He looked at the two men and smiled. "I expect these boys want to get on with things, right, boys?"

Ben managed a smile; Frank merely dropped his gaze.

Sarah knew she wouldn't have much time now. She felt in the folds of her dress for the reassuring touch of the gun. There. Yes. She wondered how she'd get the chance to draw Ben aside alone before the gunfight.

Moving away from the oak tree now, she watched as the crowd began to push for the corral and the grandstand seats.

Kerosene torches were lit and servants carried them down to the corral. The yellow flames whipped in the wind, and you could smell the kerosene burning. In their light, even attractive people looked somewhat grotesque, like beings that were not quite human. Larger torches encircled the corral. Even at dusk, the lighting here was good.

The crowd pushed up into the seats. There was a lot of drunken laughter, and meanness in the laughter. They had come, after all, to see someone shot to death.

Hollister went over and joined Adair in talking to Ben and Frank. Once again, Ben seemed attentive and interested; Frank didn't seem to be listening.

And then Sarah saw her opportunity. Ben broke from the crowd and started for the house. He likely needed to use the toilet facilities.

She noted that he went in the west wing of the house, the side hidden from the grounds being used this evening. She hurried around the back of the house; she wanted to be in position when Ben came out.

She found a gazebo that faced the west door of the place and stood flat against one side of it, so that Ben wouldn't notice her when he came out.

She took the pistol from the folds of her dress, gripping it tightly in her hand, her finger touching the trigger.

She had to make Ben listen to reason. Had to.

Frank decided to follow Adair and Hollister over to the corral. He was surprised when the scent of jasmine perfume floated on the shadows and drew close to him.

"Hello," she said, and he was surprised by how shy she sounded. He'd always been surprised by this part of her — the part that blushed at a dirty word, or was so insistent on disrobing and making love only in the dark, or that, as now, could be shy as a young girl.

"Hello."

Adair and Hollister were many paces ahead now, letting themselves be caught up by backslapping drunks.

"You mind if I say something?" she said.

"I guess not."

"I'm sorry how things turned out."

"Yeah, I bet you are."

"You never did understand me, Frank."

"Well, it's for damn sure you never understood me, either." And in that you could hear all his rage and pain. He sounded young and naive.

She grabbed his sleeve with surprising ferocity. "You stop here a minute."

"What the hell do you want?"

"I want you to come to your senses."

"Meaning what?"

"Meaning get on a horse and get out of here as fast as you can."

"Sure, Beth. And what about the ten thousand dollars you and Ben are counting on?"

"I don't care about that anymore, Frank. I just don't want to see you die."

He slid his arm around her waist, trying

to kiss her; that proved to be a mistake. "What the hell's wrong with you?"

"I don't want you, Frank, but I don't want to see you dead. It's time you changed your life and it's time I changed mine. You need to be more like Ben and I need to be more like Sarah."

"Now isn't that a sweet little speech," Frank said.

"I mean it, Frank. We both need to start acting like adults."

Then Hollister was there, one with the shadows at first, but his smile white and smirky the closer he got.

He could see they were arguing. As usual, he seemed amused by the grief of others. He was one of those people who fed on such griefs.

"Anything I can do to help?" he said.

And then Frank swung around and caught Hollister with a good, clean uppercut. He knocked the man backward, right to the edge of his heels, but before Hollister could fall on his back, Frank grabbed him again so he could hit him a few more times.

Beth screamed for him to stop, but Frank was too crazed now, the way he usually got once he hit somebody. He went over to Hollister and kicked him hard a few times in the ribs and then he pulled his boot back, ready to kick Hollister in the head.

But Beth grabbed him and knocked him off balance and wouldn't let go of him.

"Find a horse, Frank, and ride out of here fast. Please. For your sake and Sarah's. Can't you understand that?"

But fear was gone from him now, replaced with the kind of rage he could sustain for a long period. He thought of his life and how miserable it had become, and then he realized that this gunfight was an opportunity to be savored, not feared. If he lived, he'd have ten thousand dollars and could start his life over. If he lost, nothing would matter anyway.

He grabbed at her arms now and pushed her away from him.

"Leave me alone," he said.

He walked down to the corral where the torches flickered and the hard laughter of the waiting crowd could be heard.

"How much further?" Guild said.

"Up around this bend," the sheriff said. The moon had come up full now, brilliant silver and so clear you could see the configurations on its face. The night smelled of autumn, sparkling. Guild wished there were time to appreciate it. He spurred his horse.

"I sure hope we get there in time," Guild said.

When he came out of the house, Ben Rittenauer knew he needed some coffee. He needed the troubled edge it always gave him.

Shadows were deep around the house. He was surprised by how quickly it had become night. From down at the corral he could hear the sounds of the waiting crowd. Gunfights usually happened spontaneously and were the result of anger. Tonight was different. Tonight was more like a stage show. He felt nervous about it now, a little uncertain.

As he started down the sloping hill to the corral, a voice called out from behind him. "Ben."

At first he wasn't sure who had spoken. He turned to see a figure separate itself from the shadows beneath the big oak tree near a small gazebo.

The woman Sarah stepped into the moonlight. "Evening, Ben."

He knew immediately something was wrong here. He said, "Evening."

And then he saw the silver Colt she

brought up from the folds of her dress and pointed straight at him. "I asked you not to come here tonight. You're going to kill Frank."

"Maybe he'll kill me." He knew enough to stay calm, not rile her any more than she was already riled.

"You know better than that."

She came closer to him, out from beneath the tree entirely now. He hoped for a moment that she'd be close enough for him to grab, but she instinctively kept her distance.

"I'm sorry I have to do this," she said.

"You're not feeling well, Sarah. We've all been under a lot of strain."

"It's not right that she should have both of you."

"She's not a bad woman, Sarah. Just confused sometimes. The way we're all confused sometimes."

"He loves her. He can't get her out of his mind."

"I know."

"I wish he loved me that way."

"I wish he did, too, Sarah, for everybody's sake."

She was going to kill him.

He'd thought her harmless, but now suddenly he knew differently.

She was going to kill him.

They stood in the soft shadows, moonlight touching the dewy grass with silver, the scent of hay and horses strong from the nearby barn, and looked at each other.

"Why don't we see if we can go find Frank," he said.

"You're trying to trick me."

Every time she spoke, she sounded worse, crazier.

"I'm trying to help you, Sarah."

"You'll have somebody take my gun away, and then you'll go kill Frank and get the ten thousand dollars, and I'll be left with nothing."

She was starting to cry. "It's not fair."

She raised the Colt higher. Directly pointing at his heart now.

"Not fair," she said again.

Just before he threw himself to the right, he saw the Colt erupt in yellow-red fire. She cried out, but he couldn't tell what the words were and anyway he wasn't listening very well. He knew she would kill him if she got lucky with her shots, so his own gun was suddenly in his hand and he began firing, too.

He meant only to shoot her in her gun arm, to disarm her more than anything, but she stepped forward, sliding on the dewy grass, slipping away from his aim, and putting her chest where her arm had been.

In the terrible moonlight, he saw how blood bloomed on the front of her dress, and how she fell so fragile, arms waving in a horrible dance as she tumbled down, her Colt spinning from her fingers and arcing high through the air before landing on the footpath to her left.

The crowd at the corral were already shouting and running back in their direction.

Sarah was on her back on the ground, crying softly. There was no anger or fear in her now, just a gentle melancholy.

He went over and knelt next to her and said, "I'm sorry, Sarah. I didn't mean to —"

She reached up and took his hand. He held it tight for her. He did not need to hold it long.

"Sarah," he said. "Sarah."

He looked at her shuddering there on the grass, her dress soaked now, the scent of hot blood steely in his nostrils.

"Goddammit, Sarah," he said. "Goddammit. You shouldn't have tried it. He wasn't worth it and neither was I."

Behind him, a male voice said, "She's

dead, friend. She's dead."

And it was only then that Rittenauer put her hand down.

"Goddammit," he said again, though to whom and exactly about what he had no idea.

Chapter Nineteen

Five minutes later, Guild dismounted, ground-tying his animal and walked quickly to where the crowd had gathered on the side of the house. Torchlight lent the staring faces a certain forlorn quality. Here and there you could hear a woman crying.

Sheriff Carter put a big hand on Guild's shoulder. "You just stay calm, Guild, and let me handle this."

But Guild paid no attention. Inside the crowd now, he saw Frank, Beth, and Ben. He no longer had to wonder what had happened.

When he reached the front of the crowd — how pretty they smelled on the cool night air — he found her.

A small bald man in a dusty black suit bent over her. Obviously he was a doctor and obviously he was searching for vital signs, and just as obviously he was finding none.

Adair and Hollister stood on the other side of Sarah's body. The doctor looked up at them and shook his head. He closed his bag and stood up.

Guild paid the doctor no attention. He just kept staring down at Sarah. The contrast between her sweet, peaceful face and the blood spreading across her chest and stomach startling him.

Ben Rittenauer stepped up. "I'm sorry, Guild."

Guild continued to stare at her, but he spoke to Rittenauer, "You did it?"

"Yes."

"Couldn't you have goddamn shot her in the hand or something?"

"I tried, Guild. I honestly did. She had a gun on me and she moved and —"

Guild shook his head. He wished he were alone with Sarah. Finally he glanced up at Rittenauer and knew the truth. There was genuine grief in the man's face. He hadn't wanted to kill Sarah.

Two chunky Mexican men came with a stretcher and a gray woolen blanket. They forced the crowd to stand back and laid the stretcher on the dark grass and they picked Sarah up by the shoulders and the feet and then set her on the stretcher.

As Guild watched them, Frank came up.

"I'm sorry, Leo."

"I'll bet you are."

"Whatever you might think, I cared about her."

Guild turned and faced him. "You ever think that maybe this is your goddamn fault?"

Frank Evans sighed. "Leo, I didn't ask her to come out here."

"She was trying to protect you, you stupid bastard."

"I didn't ask her to protect me."

"Well, she wanted to anyway because she loved you. Doesn't that make any sense to you?"

Adair stepped into the center of the crowd. He stood on the bloody grass where Sarah had lain. "People, I'm sorry for this. It certainly isn't how I planned the evening to transpire."

The guests stood in the flapping light of the torches and the deep shadows of the evening, looking eager to forget about what they'd just seen. A gunfight between two male equals was one thing; the death of a once-pretty, older woman was quite another. She could have been their sister or mother or wife.

Adair smiled. All his arrogance was in that smile. Guild wanted to go up to him and slap him around. "But if the partici-pants are still willing, I'm ready to see a good old-fashioned gunfight. Right, Mr. Hollister?"

And with that, Hollister stepped forward with a small strongbox. Adair flipped back the lid and then held the strongbox up so everybody could see. There was no mistaking what was inside: good Yankee greenbacks.

"Ten thousand dollars," Adair said. "Ten thousand dollars to the man left standing at the end of the fight."

Ben Rittenauer looked over at Frank Evans. Between them passed a barely perceptible nod. Frank's eyes found Guild's then and dropped.

Guild said to Adair, "There won't be any gunfight tonight."

"Oh?" Adair said. "Is that right, Mr. Guild?"

"That's right. She came out here to stop it and we should at least give her that."

Beth took a small, elegant step forward and said, "Guild's right. We owe Sarah that." She looked at Ben Rittenauer. "I don't want you to fight tonight."

Adair said, speaking directly to the crowd, "I say let the invited guests decide. How does that sound, folks?"

At first only a few people applauded. But over the course of the next half minute, many others started clapping and shouting for a gunfight. Within a full minute, virtually the entire crowd was clapping and chanting, being silly in the way drunken adults are silly, eager now for activity that would make them forget the woman who'd just been killed.

"Do you hear that, Mr. Guild?" Adair had to shout above the din. "I'd say they want a gunfight."

Adair turned to Rittenauer and Evans. Hollister brought over the strongbox.

Frank Evans put out a hand and touched the money.

"Feels nice, doesn't it, Mr. Evans?"

Guild started for Adair then. If he had his way, there'd be no gunfight tonight. It was the only thing left he could do for Sarah.

But as he stepped forward to grab Adair, he felt the unmistakable shape of a gun barrel pushing into his back.

The sheriff leaned forward and said, "You're coming with me, Leo. And no goddamn argument, you understand?"

There was no sense arguing. Guild let himself be turned around and pushed back through the crowd.

The lawman took him to the far side of the house where it was quieter. They stood three feet apart. The lawman kept his Colt trained right on Guild's chest.

The first thing he said was, "Give me your gun, Leo."

The second was, "Now I want you to find your horse and get the hell out of here as fast as you can. Do you comprehend me, my friend?"

And that was when Leo hit him, a good clean shot to the side of the face, enough to knock the man to his knees, enough that Guild was able to retrieve his own Colt and hurry down to the corral where the crowd was now seating itself and where the two gunfighters were taking their places.

Unless Guild acted very quickly, the gunfight was going ahead as scheduled. He hurried through the shadows and the dewy grass.

Chapter Twenty

Tom Adair stood in the center of the corral, which now functioned as a circus ring. The huge torches set in the top boards of the corral shed a dancing, feverish light on everything inside the circle. At Adair's feet lay the strongbox, its lid open. Even from the grandstand you could see the greenbacks.

Ben Rittenauer stood at the extreme west end of the corral, Frank Evans at the east end. Both men kept their shooting hands hovering just above the handles of their weapons.

Adair said, "You all know why we're here tonight. No reason to make a speech." He waved a hand westward. "In case you didn't know, this is Ben Rittenauer." He waved eastward. "And this is Frank Evans." He folded his hands over his stomach and said, mournful as a minister now, "We had some unpleasantness a little while ago, but now I want everybody to forget that and enjoy the night." He looked to Rittenauer and then to Evans. "Gentlemen, when I give the command, draw your guns."

Guild felt someone tug on his sleeve. Beth had come up to him. The shadows from the flickering torchlight were not flattering to her and when she spoke, her voice was harsh from crying. "You've got to stop them," she said. "There's no sense in either one of them dying."

"That's just what I'm going to do," Guild said, and started to move from the side of the grandstand to the corral itself.

This time the gun barrel was pushed right into the back of his head.

"I owe you one, Leo," the sheriff said. "You turn around."

And when Guild did, the lawman hit him.

He had a good right hand, at least as good as Guild's. Guild's head slammed back against the side of the grandstand. For a moment, pinpricks of light filled his vision. He'd been hit hard.

"You said you were going to stop them," Beth said through the murk of Guild's semi-blindness.

"Nobody's stopping nobody," the lawman said.

Guild, his sight returning clearly now, rubbed his jaw and said, "I thought you were against this."

The sheriff smiled. There was no arro-gance in it, but neither was there remorse. "I have to make noises that might lead you to believe I'm against it, but actually Tom Adair is a good friend of mine."

And that was when Tom Adair shouted, "Are you ready, gentlemen?"

The crowd was silent now. They were about to see a death. They wanted to savor it.

"Ready, set, go!" Tom Adair shouted.

They started moving toward each other, Rittenauer and Evans. Their hands still hovered over the handles of their guns. Closer, closer now.

"Oh, God!" Beth said, pulling on Guild's arm like a child trying to drag her father to rescue a pet. "Can't you stop them?"

Rittenauer drew first and fastest.

The gunfire had a harsh, echoing quality on the chilling evening.

The first bullet got Frank Evans in the arm, the second in the ribs, and the third in the other arm.

He got off a few shots himself before he pitched forward, but they weren't much at all.

Ben Rittenauer walked toward the center of the corral. The strongbox was there and so was Frank Evans, facedown now.

Tom Adair and Hollister came over to Rittenauer. Adair held up Rittenauer's arm. "That was some shooting, wasn't it, folks?" he said.

The crowd showed its appreciation with applause and whistles and foot-stomping.

Beth left Guild and the sheriff and ran into the corral. In moments, she was within Ben Rittenauer's arms.

"Imagine they'll have a good time spending that money," the sheriff said.

"I imagine."

"Sorry about your ladyfriend."

"Yeah."

"She seemed decent."

"She was decent."

Adair was now holding up the strongbox and showing the contents to Rittenauer. He might have been a proud papa showing off a new infant.

The three of them stood in the center of the ring. Off to their left lay the body of Frank Evans, still facedown in the dust.

Adair was giving a speech. Maybe there was some truth to the rumor that he was considering running for office someday soon. He sure seemed to be practicing for it tonight.

"You should be a little happier now, Guild," the lawman said as the first of the people in the grandstand started down the steps toward the corral. They'd want to go over and shake Ben Rittenauer's hand and look at the corpse for themselves. There was something fascinating about a corpse.

"Why's that?" Guild said.

"Frank Evans being dead."

"I didn't want him dead."

"You didn't?"

"No, I wanted him alive and taking Sarah with him." He looked wearily at the sheriff and shook his head. "I just wanted her happy."

And that was when he saw it. One moment the body of Frank Evans was absolutely still there in the center of the corral, then the head and neck and torso of the body began angling upward.

Frank had his gun in his hand. And was pointing it.

"Watch out!" Leo Guild yelled to Rittenauer. "Watch out!"

But there was too much noise for Rittenauer to hear. And so Frank Evans got off his first shot. He shot Ben Rittenauer right in the center of the spine.

They quit talking then, of course, the crowd. Screams split the night as Frank Evans attempted to squeeze off just one more shot before death came.

That shot came just at the moment Beth threw her arms around Ben to keep him from collapsing to the ground. The bullet got Beth in the side of the head.

Guild saw her jerk with the gunshot. It was ugly, the quick harsh way she died, and he wished he hadn't seen it at all.

Guild wasn't sure who killed Evans. Somebody in the crowd had a gun and they put two shots in Frank's face. Even from here, Guild could see what a mess Evans was now.

The screaming was almost intolerable.

"Son of a bitch," Guild said.

"This is when I wish I was a railroad man or a haberdasher," the sheriff said, pushing forward to the corral. "You coming?"

"I'm taking your advice," Guild said.

"Oh?"

"I'm getting out of here fast."

The lawman frowned and shook his head. "Can't say I blame you."

There were at least half a dozen women crying now in the pandemonium in the center of the corral.

The paper lanterns Guild passed on his way back to his horse looked lonely in the night. He ducked under them and got the reins of his horse and swung up on the animal and started moving right away and as fast as possible.

Even when he was five minutes away, the darkness of the night vast and empty now, he thought he could hear them crying, the rich women standing next to the bodies.

But maybe he couldn't. Maybe the cries were just inside his head.

He spurred the horse and rode faster, faster away.